THE MIDNIGHT HOUR

THE MIDNIGHT HOUR

Benjamin Read & Laura Trinder

Chicken House

SCHOLASTIC INC. / NEW YORK

Library of Congress Cataloging-in-Publication Data available

ISBN 978-1-338-56909-4

10 9 8 7 6 5 4 3 2 1   20 21 22 23 24

Printed in the U.S.A.   23

First edition, March 2020

Book design by Christopher Stengel

For the original Emily,
my lovely Pook

–BR

For two little monsters,
Amelie and Artie

–LT

"THE IRON TONGUE OF MIDNIGHT HATH TOLD TWELVE:
LOVERS, TO BED, 'TIS ALMOST FAIRY TIME."

—WILLIAM SHAKESPEARE
A Midsummer Night's Dream
ACT V, SCENE I

CHAPTER 1

The quarter bell woke Emily in the night as Big Ben's chimes sang across the river to Lambeth and in through her bedroom window.

The streetlamps outside bleached the room a faint orange. On the wall above her bed three black glass hares chased one another in an endless circle, glinting in the light. Both her pillow and Feesh, her cuddly crocodile, were damp with tears. She levered herself up, then groaned at the red numbers on her alarm clock. Quarter to midnight, seven hours since being sent to bed forever, and she was starving.

She flopped back down on the pillow and nuzzled poor, soggy Feesh (who she only kept as a joke, and definitely didn't snuggle every night). How had this happened again? How? As always, her mom was the problem. There was just something so infuriating about her that it kept turning Emily into a human firework of foot-stamping rage. Light fuse, stand well back. Whizz, bang, pop. Huge fight. Grounded. It was totally unfair. She'd been well within her rights this time, too. Billy Jenkins from school had seen her helping her mom get something out of a dumpster, and had told everybody she lived like trash. It had made her cringe so hard there was a medical possibility that she'd never uncurl, and it was *all* her mom's fault.

According to their neighbor's most recent complaint to the council, her mom was "a crazy Irish art woman who made noise at all hours." Emily didn't disagree, but would have added "deeply shameful." If her mom didn't keep dragging her out on "special missions" to get "important art materials" *from dumpsters* to make crazy sculptures, then none of this would have happened. She wouldn't have been totally shamed at school, and she wouldn't have gotten so angry that she'd run home and ended up screaming at her mom in the kitchen about everything embarrassing she'd ever done (highlights of which included peeing behind a bush at track and field day, rescuing a lobster from a fish tank at a fancy restaurant, and once getting on the bus dressed as a horse). Emily wouldn't have made her mom cry, either. The last bit had been . . . pretty horrible. In fact, she had maybe said some things she really sort of regretted. Now she was grounded so hard by her dad she'd probably have to be homeschooled.

She would admit, if she were forced to by, like, a truth potion or something, that her big mouth hadn't helped matters. Her mom called it the "family gob," as if it was an inherited disease. If so, Emily totally had a bad case of it. When she was annoyed, or embarrassed, the gob had a mind of its own, and her mom was annoyingly embarrassing *all the time*. And that was why she hadn't said sorry, and that was why she wasn't allowed out of her room until Christmas.

Lying in the dark, the white-hot anger had faded and left behind a horrible aftertaste. Could she just lie here and not have to talk to her mom ever again? Maybe if she slipped into a coma? She was pretty hungry, though. Colossal bust-ups undoubtedly used a lot of calories. What if she raided the fridge—SNAP! The loud squeak and clatter of the big brass letter box opening and snapping shut downstairs interrupted her plans for food piracy. Who on earth was delivering things at this time of night?

There was a groaning creak from the unoiled hinges on their front gate. She sat up to peer out the window. Leaving the garden was a figure so big it was going out the gate sideways and still struggling to fit. The hulking form was holding a small black umbrella, which cast a shadow over its face. Emily pressed her nose to the window as the enormous shape squeezed out of the gate and strode off down the street with a hip-swaying walk, fancy umbrella still held high. It wasn't even raining, either. Weirdo.

She was still staring when a familiar noise chimed up from downstairs: the light, metallic almost-ring of a bell. Someone had come out of the living room and brushed past her dad's bike in the hall. He kept his big, black, bone-shaking bike there to ride to work at the post office. It was impossible to walk past it without the old brass bell dinging. More brassy notes sounded now as somebody else came into the hallway. Oh god, what was she going to say if they came up to lecture her?

It was a good time to be asleep again. She arranged herself into a very-definitely-asleep-possibly-even-comatose position and waited. The sound of an urgent conversation drifted up from the hallway, but no one came up the stairs. She lasted a whole minute, then, as a very curious person (desperately nosy, according to her mom), she slid out of bed. She picked her way through the obstacle course of books and clothes on the floor and inched the door open. She crept out onto the landing, avoiding the creaky board, snuck her head around the top of the stairs, and peeked down.

Her mom and dad were in the hallway below at the foot of the stairs, by the front door. Her mom was sitting on the bottom step wearing her long, thick coat and pulling on the big pair of spray-painted army boots she used for dumpster missions. Emily's dad was standing over her, frowning. He was holding a letter written on a sheet of thick, cream-colored paper. He had the envelope, too, a heavy, khaki-colored thing with two big, black, old-fashioned stamps in the corner. This must be what the umbrella giant had delivered. Double weirdo.

"But it doesn't make any sense, Maeve. Who delivered this? It's not midnight yet, so it can't be from the Night Post." He tapped the envelope with a stiff finger. "There's stamps on it but no postmark. It's very strange."

Her mom looked up and grinned. "Oh, and doesn't that make it all the more fascinating?" She still had a rich Irish accent despite living in London for Emily's whole life.

Her dad redoubled his frown. He read from the letter.

"'I have been asked to write to tell you that Patrick, of your clan, finds himself in grave difficulties, and would request your immediate assistance, by the code of fealty.'"

Her mom made a full eaten-something-sour face.

"Grave indeed! It's worrying about him what put Great-Auntie Aoife in hers, everybody knows it." She shook her head. "I'd best go and have a look. I'm the only one who can get any sense out of the eejit, anyway."

"But why ask *you* to come in? Surely the whole point is that you stay out? The man's a . . ."

He waved his hands, lost for words.

"Family's family, eh?" her mom said with a shrug.

Emily's ears were on fire. This was a red-alert gossip alarm going off. Her mom never, never talked about her family. *Ever.* Emily had done SO much nosing about it, and all she'd been able to get out of her was that "they didn't get on." What was that supposed to mean? Her mom just wouldn't talk about it, though. Which was unusual in itself, because she normally never shut up.

Her dad held the letter up to the light and squinted at it.

"It just doesn't smell right. The wrong post, anonymous letter, *Pat*," he said that last word like he was swearing, "wanting you to go there after all these years."

He gave her mom what Emily recognized as his most serious stare. "Are you sure it's not something to do with *her*?"

Who were they talking about? Emily was afire with curiosity (and massive nosiness).

"Ah, we saw the last of that wagon years ago," said her mom, still bent over the complicated laces of her big boots. Not somebody they liked then. "Wagon" was one of those words her mom shouted at the neighbor she was feuding with.

"Even so, it's highly suspicious. We should send a letter to the Night Watch and report it."

"Oh, we definitely should. Absolutely."

"I note you're still tying your boots up," said her dad, crossing his arms.

"Yup."

"No sign of getting a stamp."

"Nope."

"I see. Why don't I go instead when I'm at work tomorrow night?"

Her mom bounced to her feet and grabbed the letter. "Love, don't do the face, please. If Pat's in trouble, then I should be there. If it's . . . something else, then we need to know. And . . ."

Her mom grimaced and turned to look upstairs toward the bedrooms. Emily ducked back around the corner and her whole body jangled as an electric shock of nerves jolted through her. That was too close.

"I could surely do with a run right now, eh?"

Her dad let out a long, pained sigh.

"I suppose so, but you haven't been back since Emily was born. Don't let earlier . . ."

Emily inched around again. Back where? Ireland?

"It's not just that. I miss the old country sometimes, miss the job, too." Her mom sniffed as she zipped up her coat. "I even miss the clan a bit."

Her mom had a job? How had that worked? She didn't normally get up until lunchtime.

Her dad didn't say anything, but his hand squeezed her mom's arm. She looked away.

"I'm clearly not wanted around here, anyway."

"That's not true, and you know it! Think how you were at that age. The stories you've told me!"

"Ah, I was a right mare, I suppose." Her mom's usually cheerful face dropped into a dark frown Emily hadn't seen before. "I'm just not cut out for all this. I don't fit in here and I'm doing it all wrong."

"You're not. There's no right way. She's just at a difficult age."

Emily bit her knuckle so as not to give herself away by growling.

"Yeah, me too," said her mom. "Right, I'm going to stretch all my legs, find out what's going on with that eejit, and I'll be back before ye know it."

Her dad, tall against her mom, reached to open the door. He paused.

"Wait, what about the you-know-whats?" He gestured at her chest.

Eh? Was this a sports bra conversation?

"Ah, they'll be fine. I'll be in and out in three shakes of a pony's tail. I can't leave 'em here, can I?"

"Hrrrrmmm," her dad grumbled.

"Shhhh." Her mom cut him off with a finger on the lips. "I am famously uncatchable. It'll be fine."

"I caught you," he muttered past her grubby finger.

"Ye did, didn't ye? And now ye're stuck with me. Come here," her mom said, and leaned into her dad.

The distinct sounds of smooching followed. Emily ducked her head back around the corner. Some things could never be unseen. She gave it another thirty seconds to be on the safe side, then inched her head back.

They'd finished, thank goodness, and her mom was just ducking under her dad's arm to go out the door.

"If I leg it now, I can make the door at the old church before the bongs."

"Have you got your shadow key? And—"

She turned a withering glance on him, and he stopped talking, raising his hands in surrender.

"Just because I've retired doesn't mean I've gone daft."

She stepped into the night, then turned back.

"Keep an eye on the lesser horror, eh?"

Hmmph.

Her dad nodded once more and then she was gone, without a goodbye. He held the door open for a long time, just watching the dark where she had been. Emily stayed, too, until the cold air made her shiver and creep back to bed. She crawled under the covers just as Big Ben started to chime again, and the deep, resonant notes sang across the river marking the midnight hour.

CHAPTER 2

The next day was a Saturday, and the smell of bacon wafting upstairs was irresistible. Emily edged her way downstairs, past the weird scrap-metal horse's head her mom had on display in the hallway, and into the kitchen. Bacon was great, but what else was she in for? Her dad being in the kitchen was a bad sign. It was a rare sight for starters, as he'd worked the night delivery shift at the post office forever, and spent the rest of the time in the shed doing things with compost. She'd last seen him when he'd split up the thermonuclear shouting match yesterday and sent her to bed forever. She braced herself for the lecture.

"Your mother's been called away unexpectedly to a family thing. She'll be back soon and sends her love."

This was not a major telling-off. Nor was it exactly what she had overheard last night. Probably not a good time to bring that up, though . . .

"We'll say no more about yesterday, but I want you to try and be more understanding to your mom when she gets back."

Her lip curled without her meaning it to. It was a warning sign of the gob.

"And I'll ask her to do the same for you, okay? I know she's . . . a bit difficult sometimes."

This was a vastly better result than expected. The fight had been so bad that there was a chance they might have sent her off to be a chimney sweep's apprentice or something. It was all a bit too easy, though. What was going on with her mom that would make her dad overlook this?

"Is . . . is everything okay? With Mom, I mean. I didn't think she talked to her family?"

"Yes, she's fine. This was a little unexpected, but I'm sure it's fine."

He'd said "fine" twice and not answered her question. And the smile he gave didn't look quite real. She was itching to ask him more but how to do it without him finding out she'd been eavesdropping? Again. He was super cross the last time he'd found her hidden in a bush, listening in on the neighbors after reading *Harriet the Spy*. Even so, there were things she wasn't being told.

He dished up the bacon sandwiches then disappeared behind his big weekend paper, cutting off any more questions. Emily was used to this. He was always quiet, and his perfect day was one in which nothing whatsoever happened, apart from some light weeding and a pot of tea. He may actually have been clinically boring. She had absolutely no idea how he'd ended up with her mom. Maybe it was easier for him to have someone else who did all the talking? She sighed, and drowned her bacon under red sauce.

Not being able to dig about the family stuff was driving her mad. Her mom's silence about it had always been infuriating. Maybe she was on the run (potentially for crimes against fashion), or in witness protection like in the movies? The only extra info she'd ever gotten was when her mom had eaten too many bowls of a particularly strong sherry trifle last Christmas. She'd said then that the family was very traditional and had disowned her because of her choices. Emily kind of got that. There were loads of her mom's choices she didn't approve of: filling the house and garden with weird art made from trash, having multicolored hair, or talking loudly to strangers on the Tube among them. However, this was still pretty harsh. What type of people disowned their own family?

The rest of the weekend went by slower than a wheel-clamped snail. A peaceful, Mom-free house should have been paradise, but without her there to fill up all the available space with color and noise, the house was too quiet and empty. It wasn't that Emily was any less embarrassed about her mom, or less colossally furious about the dumpster incident, but . . . no old record player blaring punk, no acrid stench of spray paint drifting up the stairs; it just wasn't right. The absence of somebody normally *so* present was like the gap of a missing tooth.

School was miserable on Monday. She'd been in a foul mood and had hurt Camilla's feelings by comparing her to a sad-faced, old seaside donkey and, as a result, no one was talking to her. Again. Emily wanted to talk to her mom about it all as she was quite good at this sort of stuff, but her mom wasn't at home, and didn't have a phone. Every time she had bought one, it had blown up or died, and she'd given up in the end.

After school, Emily moped home to find her dad was back in the kitchen cooking dinner. When she asked him if he'd heard anything, he just shook his head, and kept stirring the bolognese. He forgot to put his not-quite-real smile on this time.

And that was the week. Each day she'd come home and her mom would still not be there, and her dad would be grayer and quieter. He only really knew how to cook spaghetti, so it was pasta and sadness for dinner each night. No Mom cackling about dumpster finds, or dancing in the pantry, or asking annoying questions. Who'd have ever thought she'd miss that? Instead it was just her and her dad, and a whole world of nothing to say. Each night her excuse to get out of there was going to do "homework" in her room, and she was sure he was just as relieved as she was when she left.

What was she supposed to say? When she was little he'd called her "the puzzling puppy" because she had followed him around all the time, asking questions. She'd bark at him and her mom would laugh. That was a long time ago, though, and now, without her mom to fill the gap between them with color and laughter, the right words to start talking again just wouldn't come out.

He hadn't been to work since her mom had gone. Neither of them had mentioned it, but he was definitely staying at home to make sure she was okay. As the week drew on, the words to talk to him still didn't come back, but old habits did. She definitely, absolutely, wasn't following him around, but she did read her book in the living room as he was doing the crossword, and might possibly have curled up on the grass with a comic when he was messing around with his compost heap. He was as quiet as ever, and neither of them were huggers, but now, in this Momless limbo, he would touch her on the arm as he walked past, as if to check she was still there. It was a small thing, but her arm stayed warm where his hand had rested for a long time after.

Late Sunday night, after an empty and dispiriting weekend, Emily tossed and turned and kicked the duvet off. It landed on the pile of books she'd started and abandoned that week, even their usual magic leaving her untouched. She rocked on her bed cradling Feesh the crocodile, who didn't help to fight a growing chill that had nothing to do with the heat being off. Above her on the wall, the serving plate–sized wheel of the Abbits, the moving sculpture of the three black glass hares, spun on and on in their endless chase. They ran nose to tail, their feet on the outside of the circle, their three ears pointing inward as the spokes of the wheel, a clever illusion that made it look like they all had two ears each. They were called the Abbits because she had trouble with her *R*'s when she was little. Even though her mom had told her they were hares (and she should know because she made them), Emily insisted they were called "abbits." She'd been difficult even then, apparently. Her poor mom . . . Her mom had been gone too long, and maybe (probably) it was all her fault for driving her away with her terrible gob. If her mom wasn't back tomorrow, she would pin her dad in a corner of his shed and make him tell her the truth. She would. She'd said the same thing the night before, too.

As midnight arrived the first chimes drifted over from Big Ben: one, two, three, four. She whispered the old words her mom had taught her that went along with them:

"All through this hour,

Lord be my guide;

That by thy power,

No foot shall slide."

As the first bong pealed out after the chimes, the squeak and clatter of the letter box rattled up the stairs, along with the rustle-thump of something hitting the mat. She shot straight up and jerked the curtain back. A slim, black-clad figure on a bicycle shot out from the circle of the streetlight's glare, faster than any bike she'd ever seen. Was it electric or something? She sat there in the dark. Someone had delivered something late at night again, the same as the night her mom left . . . A second later she was out of bed, hopping over piled-up books and pelting downstairs.

Emily collided with her dad coming the other way at the bottom. He caught her before she fell. Who knew he could move so fast? He kept his arm around her. On the mat at their feet lay a big brown envelope, made of a thick, waxy paper. Her dad scooped it up. On the top corner of the envelope were two more of the large black stamps. They were embossed with a skull shape and had a livid red postmark stamped over them. Written across the front, in a big sloping scrawl, was their address, and Emily's name.

"That's—" her dad began.

"Mom's handwriting," Emily finished. He took a long, hard look at the envelope and then handed it to her.

It was heavier than she'd expected, and the paper was stiff. The flap was sealed with a round, red wax blob. Her dad watched her, shifting his weight from foot to foot. She jammed a thumbnail under it and levered it open, snapping the seal in the process. Inside was a folded-over piece of paper, thick as cloth. There was something else in the bottom, but she was desperate to read the letter first. Crawling across the page, her mom's old-fashioned, drunken-spider handwriting was instantly recognizable.

The letter was classic Mom. Obscure, slightly bonkers, and with dubious spelling. It read:

Ello darl,

Sorry I had too Run. Things afoot.

Tell ye da he were right, it wasn't from Pat at all. Our old "friend" (That word had musical notes drawn round it, for some reason) *is back!*

I need to sort this out but I PROMISE I'll be back soon, I'm just not sure when.

I want you to look after sumthing fer me until I gets back. You have to Promise to Wear it for Luck the whole time.

Home as soon as I can.

Luv,

Ma

P.S. tell ye Da not to worry, he's a worrier.

P.P.S. Don't forget to feed the Hedgepigs.

It also had a useful sketch of a hedgehog with an arrow pointing to it, in case of confusion.

Emily turned the letter over, but there was nothing else.

Her dad was reading over her shoulder. He was rubbing his face, and his eyes were half closed in thought.

"I'm a worrier because you're a reckless eejit," he muttered under his breath. "I need to get in."

A week's unasked questions bubbled up, a volcano about to erupt.

"Dad? What's going on? What's she talking about?"

He didn't answer her, but, stone-faced, reached for the envelope. "Can I have that, please?"

She'd never seen him look or sound this serious before.

"Dad? What's—"

He took the envelope, dangling forgotten from her other hand, and shook it. There was a jangling sound from inside. He tipped it up over his open hand. As something glinting and metallic slid out, she could have sworn he moved his hand out of the way on purpose. The tangled metal clinked onto the floor.

"Oops," he said. "Here, you grab them. They're for you, anyway."

Her fingers recognized them before she did—rough and smooth, cool and curiously warm, clinking together as she lifted them. Her mom's necklace of old coins, the "bad pennies" as she called them. She'd worn it every day for Emily's whole life. It was a simple silver chain with thirty or so coins hung from it, all with holes punched in the middle. Emily's earliest memory was grabbing at the coins as they dangled over her. The coins were all different colors: brassy, golden, and silvered, and covered in the oddest of writings and alphabets, none of them making any sense. Her mom had worn the necklace forever, and now she'd taken it off and sent it back to her. Why?

Her dad was examining the envelope and letter carefully under the light.

"I knew something was wrong, but would she listen?" He reached a hand out to touch the handlebars on his bike and gave an exasperated sigh.

"I need to find out where this was sent from. If I could just get in tonight, but it's past midnight now and . . ."

He trailed off as he noticed her glaring at him.

"In where? What do you mean? WHERE IS SHE?"

He sighed, rubbed his chin, then sat down on the stairs and gestured for her to join him. She stayed standing up, rigid with worry.

"I'm sorry, love. It's . . . very difficult to explain, but it's all to do with your mom's old life and where she comes from."

"Ireland?"

He hesitated.

"Yes. Kind of. Pretty much." He sighed. "Her family is actually over here now, and–"

"WHAT! I thought she was in Ireland! Why hasn't she been home?"

Emily started to leak a bit at the corner of the eyes. She was absolutely *not* a crier (the other night didn't count) so it must just have been excess brain liquid or something. Her dad pulled her down onto the stairs and put his arm around her, and that made more brain juice leak out.

"Look, your mother has a very complicated relationship with her family and where she used to live . . ."

"Why hasn't she phoned?"

"They have . . . almost no phone signal there. It's a very backward part of town." He blushed as he said it. He was a terrible liar.

"It's because of me, isn't it? Because I'm horrible." She'd been thinking it for days.

He turned her around so he was eye to eye with her.

"It's not you, Puzzle, I promise, and you are not horrible. Almost never, anyway." He smiled just a little as he said that, and she nearly smiled back. "It's just your mom being her usual self. She's not famed for forward planning, is she?"

"But what's she going on about?" The whole letter was just bonkers and she was going to explode soon if she didn't get some answers.

"It's just there's so much to explain about . . . everything." He pinched his brow as he thought. Big conversations were not his specialty. "Look, we'd agreed we'd give you The Talk when you were old enough to understand, but this has all come out of nowhere . . ."

She really hoped it wasn't going to be *that* talk. Not now, not with her dad. She'd probably die.

". . . and your mother should be here for it. It's not for me to talk about her family stuff, it just wouldn't be right."

"But—"

"Please, just listen. I think your mother is currently doing something dange—unwise, something unwise. I need to go and make sure she's okay."

His face was tight and serious again. Was her mom in trouble?

"Once I go into the Night—my post office, I can speak to somebody who knows all about letters and find out where this one was sent from."

"Then what?"

"Then I find her and bring her home. When she's back, we'll sit down and talk about it all properly, I promise. Okay?"

She sniffed a particularly loud and disgusting sniff, then nodded.

"Can you go now? I don't mind being on my own."

He grimaced. "I can't. The doors to the office are locked after midnight. I'll have to wait until tomorrow now."

"Oh."

"Don't worry, there's plenty of time. Why don't I make us a hot chocolate, and you'd better feed the hedgepigs, hogs, whatever they're called."

CHAPTER 3

Emily didn't have pets. "Animals aren't things to be owned," her mom would always say whenever Emily had begged for a puppy. What she had instead was the wide and eccentric circle of things her mom fed in the garden. Birds, foxes, badgers, and her mom's favorite of all, hedgehogs. Or hedgepigs, as she insisted on calling them. Her mom would buy all types of fancy cat food for them and they would sometimes both sit out at night to watch them feed. Emily was pretty certain her mom talked to them, too, when she wasn't there. She was a big 'hog fan herself. She related to their prickly, bumbling progress and had total envy for their ability to roll into a spiky ball. How many times a week would that be useful?

She went out with the stinky cat food to load up the saucers, and there, right on their back step, was a hedgehog, half balled-up and on its side. He was breathing, the little tummy moving, but his tiny pink tongue was sticking out and he looked very under the weather. She picked him up with care and brought him back in. Her mom volunteered at Hedgehog Rescue, so this wasn't the first time she'd done this. She popped the patient in a high-sided cardboard box, made a hot-water bottle, and got one saucer with water and another with a tiny bit of cat food. The hedgehog still wasn't doing much, so she melted some honey in warm water and ever-so-slowly dripped a bit from her finger into the side of his mouth, right on the hanging-out tongue. The tongue moved, the nose wrinkled as he sniffed, and small black eyes appeared from under the folds of his face. Encouraged, she gave him a bit more, and he smacked his lips and swallowed it.

"That's it, Hog. You drink some of that."

He righted himself, and slurped some water from the saucer. He was inching over to sniff the cat food as her dad came in with the hot chocolate.

"What's this, then?"

"This is Hog. He's poorly. Is it okay if he stays in here?"

Her dad crouched down to look in the box.

"Of course. I'd never hear the end of it otherwise."

The Hog turned to look at them both and gave a little

grunt, then proceeded to curl up by the hot-water bottle and started to snore.

She took the Hog out into the garden in the morning as he'd been bumbling around okay, but he turned his nose up at the offered freedom and returned to the corner of the box. She'd been secretly glad, and he was now snug in her room and whiffing faintly of cat food and leaf mold.

By mutual unspoken agreement she hadn't gone to school but, by the end of the day, she almost wished she had. She spent all of it waiting for it to be time for her dad to go to work. She wanted him to go straight away, but his office didn't open until super late apparently. She had been very patient about the whole thing.

"But I thought you said they closed at midnight."

"They do, you have to be there just before. It's a . . . security thing."

"It's a stupid thing!"

They'd come close to an argument, the quiet, empty peace of the last week broken by last night's delivery.

She spent the rest of the day sitting in her room to avoid accidental fireworks. The gob could not be trusted when she was this wound up. The Abbits chased one another's tails above her head. It was one of the few bits of her mom's sculpture she'd ever liked. She sat and watched them spin as she toyed with the coins now hanging around her neck. The "bad pennies" were a strange new presence, and sat heavy on her. The coins were both warm and cold against her skin, and sometimes hotter or colder than she expected.

Her dad called up. "I'm going!"

She ran down and held the door for him as he wheeled the big, old bone-shaker of a bike outside. As it passed her, she reached out on impulse and rang the bell. It trilled out, brassy and bold. He smiled.

"You used to do that all the time when you were little. Drove your mom mad."

He gave her his serious look, reserved for lectures on road safety and bicycle maintenance.

"Can you just stay in the house? And don't answer the door until I'm back."

"Erm, okay."

"I'm sure it's fine, but I worry, that's all."

He kissed her on the cheek, and fuzzled her hair in a way he hadn't since she was little. She didn't even tell him off.

"I'll be back as soon as I can."

He hopped aboard and freewheeled down their street. She stayed in the doorway until he was all the way out of sight, his red bike light disappearing into the darkness. She shut the

door and, after a pause, double-locked it before she went
to bed.

Her dad did not come back in the morning. He did not, in
fact, come back all that day or that night. She had phoned
him again and again, but it didn't ring out, or go to voice mail,
it just made a peculiar beeping noise, then a sticky screech, as
if he was abroad or in outer space or something. She hadn't
gone to school again the next day, but waited at home in the
hope he'd return. That night she sat up late with the Hog on
her lap, despite being pretty sure he had fleas, and scratched
his nose and pretended it was going to be all right. Her dad
was going to come back, and bring her mom with him. Any
minute now. She played one of her mom's old punk records so
the house wouldn't be too quiet, and fell asleep sitting up and
still dressed.

Now, the day after, she had to admit it: Her dad was missing, too. Something had happened to him the same way
something had happened to her mom. The sensible thing to
do was phone the police.

She was halfway to the phone when it dawned on her she
wasn't old enough to be on her own. If she told the police, or
anybody, they'd ask her if she had any relatives, and she'd

have to say "none she knew anything about," and then they'd take her away in a van to reform school, or whatever it was they did to semi-orphans. That was if her school didn't send somebody first. They had already left two messages saying something about unexplained absence and truancy officers. What was she going to do? Someone was going to find out and take her away. But who would wait here in case her mom and dad came back? Who would look after the Hog?

She slumped onto the little seat beside the phone in the hallway and leaned back into the coats hung above it. As she did, her mom's perfume of spray paint and varnish wafted out of her old bomber jacket, and her dad's gardening coat gave out a cloud of greenhouse and bonfire. She leaned farther in and breathed it deep. As she did, the gate clicked outside and she sat up. It must be her dad! She was halfway up to open the door for him when she was gripped by a horrid vision. What if it was the truancy officer? Through the frosted glass of the front door, a blurry figure approached the house. It was tall and thin, with a cap and a bright-red scarf. Whoever it was, it wasn't her dad. She sank back into the coats and stayed still. The figure rang the bell, then rapped the letter box, too.

"Hellooo, is the gentleman of the house here? It's really quite important, so it is."

He had a rich, rolling Irish brogue, creamy with charm.

He rang the doorbell again and banged the letter box hard. He pressed himself close to the glass, his black shape filling it.

"I'm on officially business-like and all that. I have to discuss yer family situation with ye."

Emily was close to being sick in her lap. He WAS an inspector.

"Helloo? I'm a very important message. I mean, I have a very important massage, relating to yer daughter and going you-know-where."

That was it, they were going to put her in the van. The man leaned his head against the glass, and through it the shadows made his face a skull.

"Why aren't ye here? I'm definitely not late. I'll grant there was a certain sense of urgency in the original instruction . . . but it's clearly not my fault."

What?

"Helloo? This is very inconvenient for me, y'know? I made certain commitments, regarding the delivery of this massage. Under fierce duress, I might add. She's a vicious mare, she is. Begging your pardon obviously."

His head moved against the frosted glass, the prism splitting his outline into a thousand different shapes.

"I definitely didn't go to the pub on the way, no matter what ye might hear." He paused. "Oh jaysus, he's already gone in, hasn't he?"

What was he talking about? She inched forward on the seat, and his head snapped up.

"Is someone there? Helloo?"

He disappeared from view. A grimy-fingered hand lifted up the letter-box flap, and a beady eye was pressed to it. She gasped and jammed herself back into the coats.

"Would that be the wee lady of the house? Are ye the daughter? Is that it?"

Emily didn't dare breathe.

"Have they both gone and left ye? Ye positively shouldn't be there on yer own. Absolutely not. It's a terrible idea."

She squeezed herself so still she might never unclench again.

"Ye should probably come with me. Maybe just open the door and we can have a chat about it all, eh? It's all fine, I know yer ma and da."

Emily was very glad she'd double-locked the door after her dad's parting words, but it was a thin barrier between her and this odd, odd man.

"Helloo? Little girl? Oh, this isn't helping, and I've a terrible head from last night, I really do."

He sighed.

"Look, if ye are in there, ye shouldn't be on your own. It won't be me next comes to yer door, that's all I'm saying. It'll be something worse."

The letter box creaked shut and he reappeared at the glass.

"Nothing? Honestly? Right, well, I've done me best, anyone would agree."

His shadow disappeared from the door, and a fluting whistle struck up from outside as the front gate clicked shut behind him.

Emily sagged forward as the whistle moved off down the street, interrupted by a hacking smoker's cough. She was as horrid and sweaty as if she'd just run a marathon. Who were they going to send around next? There was no way she was going to sit here and wait to be taken away. She'd just have to go and find her mom and dad herself.

Emily put her sensible head on and worked it out. She had no idea where her mom was, but her dad had gone to the post depot. She'd go there first, then, although not until late tonight. What kind of stupid place only opened just before midnight? What did she need in the meanwhile? Sandwiches, of course. "Never be knowingly under-snacked" was her mom's motto. She whipped up a couple of subs in the kitchen and popped them in a paper bag. She took them upstairs with her, along with some cans of soda, and, emptying her school backpack out, started filling it with useful things: phone, bus pass, wallet (empty). She'd better get some cash, too.

She ran back downstairs into her dad's tiny study, filled only with a desk and a stack of gardening books. She pulled the drawer open, and amid the pencils, rubber bands, and seed catalogs was a pile of change he kept there. Next to it was a canvas pouch, with a Post-it note on it in her dad's neat handwriting, marked "Just In Case." She picked it up, and a flash of vivid color gleamed below it. It was a neat, see-through plastic folder with two huge stamps the size of coasters, glistening ruby-red, each with a picture of an angry woman wearing a crown on it. Beneath the red stamps was a sheet of smaller black skull stamps, the same as the ones on the letter from her mom. Her dad was a stamp collector? That figured. If she dug deeper in his desk, she'd doubtless find a book on trainspotting, too.

She started to rummage in the just-in-case bag. Inside was an unusual assortment of items: a colorful wad of big paper money like foreign banknotes, which on closer inspection were just very old British ones; an old library card in her mom's maiden name, Connolly. She paused there; her crazy, chatty mom in a library? It was a baffling image. There was also a tatty leather wallet containing a badge for Her Majesty's Night Post. The coat of arms was the same as on the black stamps: a skull over crossed scrolls tied with ribbons. Tucked inside the wallet was an ornate key, whose fob had the same skull design on it. Emily gave a long-suffering sigh.

Just in case of what? She shook her head. Her parents were idiots and she'd have to sort it all out herself. She took the whole pouch with her, anyway, just in case, and pocketed the change.

Bag packed, she went to get the Hog.

"Hoggins? Where are you? It's time for you to go back out."

He was not in his box. He wasn't under the bed or behind the wardrobe, either. She filled his saucer with water, and gave up. She was going to miss her bus if she wasn't careful.

"You better not poo everywhere!"

She pulled her biggest, clompiest pair of boots out from the back of the wardrobe, and laced them to the top. She didn't wear them often because they were a bit mom-ish, but, "Big boots are best." Another one of her mom's sayings. As she came downstairs, she reached for her duffle coat, hesitated, then shrugged and grabbed her mom's tattered bomber jacket instead. There was another waft of spray-paint perfume as she slipped her arms into the bright-orange interior, and she smiled. She pulled her backpack on, patted the necklace of coins through layers of clothes, and went out the back door into the dark.

She slipped out the back gate along the thin passage known as Dog Poo Alley, and back out onto her own street, but way up from the house and right by the nearest bus stop.

Total secret-agent move, just like in one of her books. The bus would be here any minute and take her over the Thames and to the depot in central London in plenty of time for midnight. This whole late-night-mission thing was quite exciting, actually.

As she waited, something caught her eye. Way back up the street past her house was a man, a very big man, pounding along, holding a petite black umbrella above his head, despite it being dry. Huge . . . umbrella . . . it was the man who'd delivered the letter that had taken her mom away! This was perfect, she'd get some answers out of him if she had to bash him with his own umbrella.

She was about to shout at him, when she stopped. What was he doing? He stood in the street and moved his big head from side to side and . . . was he sniffing? Even from this far away, she could hear the great gulping snotty intakes of air echoing down the street as he snorted. He towered over the front hedges, which must have made him . . . seven feet tall? That was never right. He was big, but not fat, despite being large enough to have swallowed a small car. He walked with a slow, muscular stride, and a loping rhythm. He had short legs, and old-fashioned clothes: a tweed suit, gray and fuzzy, stretched tight over the shoulders, tummy, and butt, straining as he moved.

His face was still hidden. There was a shadow under the

umbrella that was deeper than it should have been, covering him in darkness. Something just wasn't right about him, and she didn't want to ask him any questions after all, she decided. As he came level with her house, he stopped and sniffed again, harder and harder, his big head moving around, nosing something out. He put a great, hairy hand on her gate and she gave an involuntary yelp. She clapped a hand over her mouth but it was too late. It should have been impossible for him to hear her from there, but his head whipped around and he stared down the street toward where she stood. He took one final, long sniff, then started to stride toward her. She wanted to turn and run, but ice filled her chest and her feet just wouldn't move. As he drew ever closer something glinted under the umbrella's shadow. He was grinning with sharp, white teeth.

CHAPTER 4

Are you getting on or what?"

The bus driver's grumpy voice broke the spell. The bus had pulled up alongside her. The door was open and the driver was glaring at her.

"Oh yes, please!"

She hurled herself through the doors, and they hissed closed behind her. She stumbled toward him, bus pass in her hand.

"Please go, quickly."

He scowled but pulled away from the bus stop. The huge man was running down toward her now, thundering along far faster than he looked capable of. He only stopped as the bus accelerated off past him down the road.

"Too late, mate," muttered the driver.

The man raised a huge hand and pointed straight at her, until the bus turned a corner and he vanished from view. She slumped back into a seat and put her face in her hands.

She rocked there for a while, stiff with fright. What had just happened? Also, why was she starving? She added "fear" to the long list of things that made her hungry, and tugged her bag open to root around for an emergency sandwich.

"OW!" She yanked her hand back out and sucked the end of her finger. Something sharp had stuck straight up under the nail. "What the heck?" She peered in the bag, muffling a scream when something moved inside. There was a shuffling and a grunting noise, and then a small black nose appeared, followed by a brown, sleepy face.

"HOG! What are you doing in there? You're very naughty."

She cupped her palm and his small-footed weight filled her hand with warmth. She held him up, grinning and cooing over him. The old lady on the other side of the aisle was not as pleased. She got up and moved away, giving them both a dirty look. Who cared? Look what a nice nose her spiky stow-away had.

"Something very scary just happened, Hoggins. I'm glad you're here." The Hog did not respond, but wriggled with pleasure at the nose rub.

She squeezed him (not too tight) and he tucked in under

her chin. The streetlamps and headlights streamed by as the bus took them into the city.

"Wait, have you been eating my sandwiches, you little git?"

Half an hour later, and now far too close to midnight, Emily still hadn't found the post office, which was just ridiculous. She knew where it was. Her dad had mentioned it lots of times. St. Martin's Le Grand, right in the middle of the city, where he'd cycle in, no matter what the weather. St. Martin's was easy enough to find; it was a big built-up area right by St. Paul's, a mix of shiny new offices and huge old buildings. What it didn't have was any sign of a post office. It should have been simple; her dad had always made it sound huge. Yet she'd gone around the whole block, and there was nothing but bankers' offices and coffee shops. There was just no sign of it. She was back out on the corner of Foster Lane and Cheapside now, clearly too young to be out on her own at this time of night and getting funny looks from late-night revelers staggering home. She kicked a lamppost and hurt her toe, even through the big boots. She searched on her phone and found first a Postman's Park, and then . . . a post office right where she was! The burst of hope died; it had been demolished in 1912.

But he'd said it was here. He'd even talked about the loading bay. She stood there, nose running from the cold breeze, while the glass-fronted buildings towered over her and gave no answer. Had her dad lied to her all this time? Was Night Postman even a real job? She had just pictured him delivering mail late at night. That did sound a bit off, now she came to think about it. But if her dad wasn't a postman, where had he been going every night? Was he one of those people who pretended to still have a job because they didn't want to tell people they'd been fired? He'd been going there her whole life, though, and all those cardigans and copies of *Gardeners' Weekly* weren't going to pay for themselves. She wiped her nose on her sleeve and went to walk around one more time. She didn't have a single idea of what to do next if she couldn't find it.

She turned up Foster Lane again. Maybe she'd missed something at the back of the big modern building that was sitting on top of where the old post office must have been? She shoved her hands in her pockets, cupping one of them over a snoozing Hog for warmth. His little snores buzzed through her fingers.

"Girl."

Emily lurched as the voice boomed behind her. It was a gritty roar of a voice, like a big engine or a wild animal. She didn't want to turn around, she really didn't. There, at the mouth of the lane, on the other side of the road, the streetlights silhouetted a huge figure. It was impossible to make out a face, but its bulk would have been enough of a giveaway, even if it wasn't topped off with the perfect outline of a small umbrella. It was the terrifying man. How was he here?

"I smell you, girl," he growled as if reading her mind. "You reek of sorrow, paint, and ill luck. Easy to follow, even in this stinking place."

She was hunched over out of sheer fear. The very sound of his voice paralyzed her again. He hadn't done anything, and that umbrella was ridiculous, but something deep inside her was screaming that he was as bad as could be.

"I–I . . ." Her throat seized up. A thick, musky odor filled the air, all raw meat and blood. He walked toward her, crossing the empty road, and still her legs were locked in place.

"I take you now. Mistress will be pleased. You stay there, little rabbit." His voice grizzled lower, a chainsaw symphony, as he crooned at her to keep her still. He stepped into the light coming from a coffee-shop sign, and it cut into the dark under the umbrella, revealing a broad protruding nose, deep-set dark eyes, and a thick black beard that covered most of his face and neck. He filled the pavement, half as broad as he was tall, a boulder of a man rolling toward her.

"Come with me, can see your mother, girl."

Mother? The shock unglued Emily's feet. She turned and ran, head down and hare fast, pelting down the empty road ahead. Behind her came an awful inhuman roar, and then the thudding of heavy running feet. This was bad, this was bad, this was BAD.

She panted and hurtled and skidded but, fueled by sheer terror, gained and kept a good distance over him. It was a long, straight road, though, and she'd seen him run *very* fast toward the bus stop. She passed an old church, then spotted a tiny alley on her right and, letting instinct guide her, shot down it. The entrance arch was stone and wood, one of those little reminders of London's history you saw everywhere. The alley was small and bendy, like her. She would get down here faster than the terrible-voiced man. As she ran, the coins worked their way from under her T-shirt, and jingled up and down in time with her pumping legs. She zigged to the right as the alley turned, hurtled straight into a small courtyard, and . . . ran out of road. Twenty yards in front of her was a pile of traffic cones and orange barriers and tape blocking the exit. "CLOSED FOR REFURBISHMENT WORK–SORRY FOR ANY INCONVENIENCE."

She skidded to a halt and looked around, frantic. The alleyway was all dark brick and guttering and . . . a door. She ran to it, slamming into it as she failed to slow down. It was an old wooden door with a brass plaque on it. There, under a stylized engraved picture of a skull over scrolls, were the words: "THE NIGHT POST." *Oh, now she found it!*

She grabbed the handle and yanked at it with no effect. She hammered on the door, her hands smarting with pain, and shouted for help. Her voice was swallowed up by the dark, and nobody came.

"Why are you locked?" she shouted, and then a bolt of lightning lit up her brain! Skulls! Skull on plaque was the same as skull on key in wallet; therefore key might unlock door! She squeaked a noise only dogs could hear, and grabbed at her bag, scrabbling to get into the front pocket.

Behind her, not far away, a low growl rippled down the alley. "Better when they run."

Nothing could have made her turn around. She jammed her hand into the pouch and clawed through the stuff: old money, the wallet, and *there*, the key! She yanked it out and fumbled it the right way around, as colorful bank notes drifted to the floor.

"But nowhere left to go." The deepest voice in the world was closer now. She jammed the key in the lock and turned it and . . . nothing. It wouldn't turn, it didn't fit, the door stayed locked. She was toast.

She had to look. The huge man stood back down the alley by the entrance to the courtyard, not even breathing hard. Under the pitch-dark of the umbrella, his sharp-toothed grin glinted.

"So now . . ." he said and lowered the umbrella to his side.

His grin grew wider and wider, stretching out and around the sides of his head, as giant white teeth pushed out to fill it. His face started to ripple and change, nose projecting forward, his beard squirming up to cover the rest of his cheeks and around his eyes, his hair pushing down from the top of his head to meet it. He grew larger and threw his arms back, his hands now covered in hair and tipped with razor claws. A moment later, his huge hairy chest burst through his over-strained shirt.

His vast paw, because it was a paw now, came up and pointed at Emily as it had earlier.

"Mine," he said, his words now a growl from the jaws of a *bear.*

She couldn't move. Not a muscle. The bear-thing grinned and dropped forward onto his paws, arched his back, and roared. If Emily hadn't been to the bathroom before leaving the house, there'd have been an embarrassing accident right there and then.

She sobbed. The creature filled the whole alley, grinning, playing with her, and enjoying her fear. He was somewhere between man and bear now, face that of the beast and down on all fours but still draped in tweed, with shoes on his hind legs. He was grotesque, ridiculous even, but still the worst thing she had ever seen.

CHAPTER 5

Emily pressed her face against the unyielding door and closed her eyes. As she did, the first of the midnight chimes from Big Ben drifted up the Thames and across the city. The key, still gripped tightly in her hand, turned just a tiny bit. She hissed like a cat, and grabbed it in both hands, twisting the key so hard it bit into her fingers.

"Oh, please!"

As the delicate chimes finished, and the first big bong sounded, the key clicked and turned, as smoothly as if it had been greased. With her full weight on it, the door swung inward and she fell through. The Bear roared behind her and charged forward, faster than something that big should have been able to move. She yanked the key out of the lock and, scrambling around, threw herself against the door and slammed it. It banged into the frame and, shaking now with pure panic, she managed to fumble the key back into the door and lock it just as the Bear hit. There was an awful impact, and the whole wall shuddered. Any moment the door was going to fall through and the Bear was going to land on her. But it held. There was another vast thud, and another, but the door budged only a fraction and held firm. A horrendous howl of rage came from the other side.

"Good door, good door," she muttered, then, as the Bear hurled himself at it again, she squealed and shot down the corridor behind her, into the darkness.

Emily ran, bouncing pell-mell off walls and corners, zigzagging into the heart of the building. The storm of the Bear's terrible anger faded behind her, although it might have been the sound of her pounding heart drowning it out. A faint light shone ahead and she slowed to a halt. She clawed down the zipper of the bomber jacket and stood there panting, soaked with fear-sweat and reeking nearly as bad as the Bear had. She was not a fan of sudden, unprovoked exercise at the best of times, and this had been two Olympic sprints in short succession. She slumped against the wall and gulped in air. Was a giant, murderous bear-thing stalking her in the dark? She'd have heard the door crash in, wouldn't she? But there had been a lot of running just now. Was he in here? WHAT THE HECK WAS HE?

She pulled herself to her feet and staggered on. She was as sick as a . . . what was always being sick? Dogs? They did throw up a lot. But so did cats. Sick as a . . . wait. Was this what being in shock felt like?

She reached into her bag and opened and chugged a whole can of fizzy soda as she walked. She burped long and loud afterward and the wobbles cleared. She checked on the Hog but he had slept through the whole marathon of terror. What had just happened? Something properly not explainable, something deeply weird. What had that thing been, a were-bear or something? His words rang in her ears, *"Come with me, can see your mother,"* and she bit her lip, hard. Whatever he/it was, it had something to do with her mom being missing.

At least she'd managed to find the Night Post. On her own, too. She'd find her dad next, and everything would be fine.

The light in the corridor was creeping out from under a door marked "Staff Only." Behind it there was a locker room of sorts, with long oak benches and tall wooden cabinets. They had little tags with extraordinary names on them:

"Moves-silently-by-night," "Fortescue Bloodfang," "Vermillion Eve" . . . And there! Her own name, "Featherhaugh." Her name was a total pain because of having to explain *every time* how to spell or say it (Fevver-oh), but here it made her smile. Her dad must be here somewhere. At the far end of the locker room was a double door, and a hum of activity and voices became louder as she walked toward it. She ran a finger under the neck of her T-shirt and touched the body-warmed edges of the bad pennies for luck, then inched the door open and slipped through.

It led into a huge, high-ceilinged space filled with a whirl of activity and noise. It was some kind of mail-sorting room but it wasn't a modern one; there were no conveyor belts, machines, or bright lights. Instead there were stack upon stack of wooden pigeonholes, and teetering shelves, and ladders balanced between them. It was lit from above with brass-fitted gas lamps, shining down on sorting desks with pneumatic tubes at the back of them, rattling and hissing and thumping as they pumped out more and more letters and parcels onto desks already mounded high with them.

The post, oh the post. Rivers of it flowed past her and as she stood there, more mail poured in: from the tubes, dumb-waiter hatches, and on trolleys from some hidden back room. The letters were in the same sort of envelopes that had been delivered to her house, with wax seals on brown paper, and colored inks galore. They were everywhere, incalculable numbers of them, outweighed only by the parcels. Packages of every shape and size were stacked in piles, wrapped in silk, or carpet, or paper, tied up with string, ribbon, rope, and . . . snakes? A lot of them moved, rocking, hopping, gyrating, and in some cases, making a determined bid for escape. She was pretty sure one of them was a live crocodile, gift-wrapped in shiny paper with a fancy bow. That wasn't right, was it?

Her head was spinning. The hypnotic flow of mail was one thing, but the people who were handling it all were just as strange. The postal workers were all dressed in stiff, gray, long-tailed jackets and striped trousers, or high-necked dresses, and the men (well, mainly the men) had immense mustaches. It was all a bit period-drama. They were in constant motion, rolling on wheeled chairs, climbing up shelves, staggering under the weight of letters, and chasing parcels with butterfly nets. One lunatic was using steam-powered roller skates to move quicker. They whirled around the floor in a complicated ballet of movement, sometimes crashing into one another and sending a plume of letters up into the air.

The letters sometimes didn't come back down because, above the sorting room floor, the air was thronged with bats and crows swooping back and forth with letters gripped in claws or beaks. Were some of those letters flying on their own? They were. Oh good. Perfectly normal. Perhaps it might be time for a sit-down somewhere quiet? Magic post office, shape-changing bear ... was she losing the plot? Below the desks came a flickering movement, then two rats in tiny hats ran past her, dragging a parcel on a little sled. Right, that was quite enough, thank you. They were all crazy, and it was impossible. She must have banged her head.

Fixated on their own work, no one paid the slightest bit of attention to Emily, even when they walked right by her. They were all piled up with stacks of letters, or wrestling with squirming parcels. She turned around and around, eyes wide with shock. What was this place? Where did her quiet and boring dad fit into all this madness?

Everyone, including Emily, jumped as a steam whistle blew an ear-rattlingly loud and shrill note. After it, an amplified voice, dry and brittle as fallen leaves but still loud enough to part hair and chill bone, yelled, "Two-minute warning. Two-minute warning, until the Night Post rides out!"

The mayhem intensified. People threw parcels with total abandon, fountains of mail gushed into the air, and stacks of letters toppled from baskets as their handlers ran for it.

Perhaps there was some method to the madness after all? The post was moving toward the far end of the room, where, in front of huge sliding warehouse doors, a row of mismatched vehicles stood in a loading bay. There was a steamroller with a huge seat, a massive white horse loaded with saddlebags, a small sled harnessed to . . . were those wolves? Then at the end was a row of big black bicycles with panniers, the same as her dad's. The same as her dad's! Was he still here?

Next to the fleet of post vehicles were the posties themselves. They wore a different uniform from the rest: all black with glinting silver bits, and a jaunty peaked cap. Some were human, if a bit pale, but farther down the line was a wolfish chap, another with tentacles, and toward the far end, a glimpse of a graceful creature, face covered in soft white feathers. At the end of the line, a slim figure, facing away from her. Her dad! She was almost sure. Why was he still here at work days later? In this absolute madhouse, too. Her mom was missing, she'd come close to being a bear snack, and he was here bagging mail with a bunch of Halloween rejects? Not cool. She started to shoulder through the crowd to get to him, but it was difficult to get closer in the whirling bedlam.

She pushed and shoved, catching glimpses of the posties loading their vehicles. They were all taking the letters, packages, and wriggling parcels that were being handed to them and jamming them into the panniers, baskets, and shoulder bags as fast as they could. She saw something the size of a hatstand go into a carpetbag the size of a briefcase. Every single person on the floor now kept glancing up at an iron balcony that ran the length of one wall and overlooked the loading bay. Sticking over the edge was the end of an enormous brass megaphone, from which came another shriek in that nasty voice: "ONE-MINUTE WARNING!"

The movements below became more frantic, and eruptions, accidents, and droppages became more pronounced. As the seconds ticked away, the frenzy on the floor reached a climax. The whole line of posties sat astride their different steeds now, and every one of them was staring at the huge doors of the loading bay, jockeys waiting for the starting gun.

She was so close to them now, so close to the figure that just had to be her dad. She yelled to him but as she did the awful whistle blew again. The wolfy postie clutched his ears with big hairy hands and howled, and she was drowned out. With a great creak, the doors slid open, moonlight silvered in, and the dry voice screeched over the mayhem.

"NOW! THE NIGHT POST RIDES OUT!"

CHAPTER 6

The fleet of posties, large and small, winged and wheeled, furred and feathered, surged for the doors in a wave of black and silver. Emily yelled as loud as the megaphone. "Dad!"

The slim figure she'd been so close to turned around. It wasn't her dad, not unless he'd grown scales and big eyes, chameleon-style. A forked tongue flickered out of its mouth, and then the green-faced lizard postie turned back and began to pedal with all the rest. In a bedlam of bells ringing, crows squawking, and steam whistles blowing, they pedaled and galloped and whooped and swooped, and hurtled out of the doors and into the night.

She stood there as they arced up into the sky. Flying bikes.

Yeah, sure, why not? She sagged, empty. The whole place had gone quiet. The dreadful voice came again from above.

"Start the tidy-up immediately. Prepare the next shift! And who is *that* in the middle of the loading bay? SEIZE THE TRESPASSER!"

The whole room went quiet, and all eyes turned to Emily. "Ah," she said.

"Are those TROUSERS?"

Emily had surrendered. A tall, regal black woman, dressed in an old-fashioned gray dress, led her upstairs. She had, at least, smiled before pointing the way. That hadn't been particularly comforting, as her teeth were pointy, and her eyes were bloodred, but it was the thought that counted. The reception on the balcony was less friendly.

"They *are* trousers! On a girl! Are you one of those ghastly progressives?"

The horrible creaking shout came from the dark at the end of the balcony. In the shadows was a desk, and behind it sat what must once have been a man. Both desk and man were covered in a century of cobwebs, dust, and in the case of the desk, mound upon mound of paperwork. The man himself was gray, withered, and so dried up that Emily would have thought he was dead if it hadn't been for the awful shouting.

His skin was shriveled and worn, his hair and beard so long and tangled they wrapped all around the chair he was sitting in and into the shelves of mail behind him. She'd have bet money he'd been there at least a hundred years, if not more. The enormous brass megaphone he had been yelling the countdown through was attached to the desk in front of him, and was now swiveled to point straight at Emily.

"No, I'm–" started Emily, but didn't get far.

"I thought all that nonsense had left the world when the DREADFUL DAYLIGHT did." Dust shot out the end of the megaphone, and the sheer volume made Emily's cheeks quiver. He didn't move an inch despite the ranting, which was totally creepy. Wait, was that a twitch, or . . . was that something else? A mouse emerged from under the hair, sniffed the air and went back in. There was another movement under his shirt, and in his hair, and . . . he was rippling with them. Were they going in and out of his clothes, or in and out of . . . him? Urgh.

"Well," said the scarlet-eyed woman in a surprisingly posh accent, "We don't all think it was dreadfu–"

"SILENCE!" The megaphone screech made Emily flinch. "I'll have no pro-daysie sedition here or you'll be out on your ear, Miss Rhowse!"

Miss Rhowse folded her arms and looked straight down her nose at the ranting corpse. Her eyes flared red.

"Is that so, Postmaster? Good luck finding anything in the files ever again, if you do."

Emily liked Miss Rhowse, scary eyes or not. She tried again.

"Look, Mr. Postmaster, sir, I'm just trying to find—"

"How did you get into MY POST OFFICE?"

"I'm trying to TELL YOU!" Emily shouted, not as loud as the megaphone but enough to stir his cobwebs. "I'm looking for my dad, who came here to find my mom. I thought he worked here but I . . . I must have made a mistake."

She ferreted in her bag and slapped the wallet and badge down on the desk. The Postmaster didn't move, although one of his eyes bulged (but it might have been a mouse moving behind it). Miss Rhowse picked the badge up. She turned it over in her hands, then held it up for the Postmaster to see. She turned back to Emily, scarlet eyes wide open with interest.

"Where ever did you get this, miss?"

"It's my dad's. I came in with his key and—"

Before she could say anything else, there was a hissing sound and a plume of dust shuddered out of the Postmaster.

"She's a DAYSIE! An illegal daysie in my post office! Worse, she's an associate of a SEDITIOUS DAYSIE WHO DESERTED HIS POST!"

Emily coughed as the cloud of dust enveloped her. Miss Rhowse waved a hand in front of her.

"Alan's not a deserter. He must have had a good reas—"

"Alan? You know my dad?" Emily blurted.

Miss Rhowse turned to her with a sympathetic, if pointy, smile.

"Yes, dear, he—"

"SAY NOTHING, MISS RHOWSE. It's a conspiracy! I shall telegraph to the Night Watch forthwith and have this ILLEGAL dealt with."

His withered hand detached itself from his wrist and crept spiderlike across the desk. Emily came close to screaming, but settled for staring, bug-eyed, instead. The spider-hand unearthed a battered contraption of brass and steel from underneath the dusty letters, then mounted it and started to tap out a message in a series of clacks and clatters.

"But, sir?" said Miss Rhowse.

"NOTHING!" Emily and Miss Rhowse both winced in the blast. "Now, escort her to a holding cell, and set a guard!"

Miss Rhowse gave him a stare that would have been withering if he hadn't already been a prune.

"We're a post office, sir. We don't have holding cells."

"Then tie her up!"

Miss Rhowse sighed.

"As you say, Postmaster."

She turned around and, with her back to the Postmaster, winked at Emily.

"Come along, miss. We need to get you tied up."

"TIGHTLY!" yelled the Postmaster after them.

She held a hand out and Emily, with no choice, took it. It was cold as winter but gave hers an encouraging squeeze.

"Drink up; you've had a nasty shock."

Emily took a long slurp of the tea she'd been handed and grabbed a biscuit from the box. She leaned back in the comfy tartan armchair by the small tiled stove in Miss Rhowse's cozy little office.

"Ta. So, he was horrible."

"Ah, he has a good heart." Miss Rhowse was perched on the corner of her desk, cup and saucer in hand.

"Yeah?" Emily narrowed her eyes.

"Oh yes, he keeps it in a jar on his desk." Miss Rhowse frowned. "But he's a blinkered bigot when it comes to the Day Folk, I'm afraid, as are so many here . . ."

"Look, Miss Rhowse."

"Please, call me Japonica."

"Okay, Japonica. Wow, cool name. I'm Emily. I . . . I have SO many questions, but I need to find my dad first." She grabbed another biscuit to see her through this difficult time. "Is he here?"

Miss Rhowse, Japonica, frowned again. It was a worrying

sight, as her thick eyebrows hovered over her bright-red eyes, and a small fang jutted out of the bottom of her mouth.

"He was. He'd missed a number of shifts then ran in one night and raced straight out of here on his delivery bike instead of doing his rounds. It's quite the scandal. The Postmaster is furious."

"My dad caused a scandal?" She'd have bet she was past being surprised, but apparently not.

"Yes, it's known as 'deserting your post,' and very bad form. Now his dangerous parcels are piling up, eating the other mail, and causing chaos. It's most out of character for Alan."

People in this crazy place knew her dad on a first-name basis. Just so weird.

"Okay, that's, that's too much right now." She pinched the bridge of her nose and squinted as she tried to wrangle her tattered thoughts into shape. "But he's been here. I'll phone him again," said Emily.

She pulled her battered phone out of her pocket and shrieked as it burned red-hot against her fingers. She juggled it then dropped it on the rug. The screen was black and charred and the whole phone was fizzing.

"Oh, is that one of your galvanic devices? How interesting." Miss Rhowse leaned in, fascinated. "I'm afraid they don't work in here. Something to do with the level of ambient magic."

Emily took a deep breath, leaned back to contemplate the ceiling, then leaned forward again.

"Okay, I give up. Magic. Monsters. Everyone being all . . . spooky?"

Miss Rhowse nodded gravely for her to continue.

"If you don't explain all this, I'm afraid I'm going to have to jump up and down and scream forever."

Before Japonica could reply, a blast of noise erupted somewhere far off in the post office. It was difficult to make any sense of it, but it might have been an angry withered man shrieking "Miss Rhowse" into a brass megaphone, again and again. Japonica's frown deepened, and she stood up, motioning Emily to her feet.

"Well, it's easier if I show you, anyway." Japonica already had the door open and was glancing down the corridor.

"What's going on?" said Emily.

"Oh, it's just the Night Watch come to arrest you for being an illegal immigrant. Chop chop, do come along."

As Japonica slipped out, Emily grabbed a handful of biscuits and shoved them in her pocket. Better safe than sorry. As she hurried after Japonica, there was a tiny munching noise.

"Damn it, Hog, those are mine."

Miss Japonica Rhowse led her out of the office, down a gas-lit corridor, and up flight after flight of steps. At the top they ducked out of a small, square door and onto the vast, flat roof of the building, which was dotted with skylights and finished in lead. Above them, the biggest and fullest moon she had ever seen. It was a hole carved out of the night and filled with mercury, and she was sure it hadn't been there when she left home earlier. She was used to living under the sour orange dome of London's reflected light and thought that was just how the sky was, but oh, how wrong she had been. The real night sky was black as a sea of ink and rippling with stars. Just so many stars, spread out in whirls of stark light, and deepening further and further, with color blooming in the darkness. Was this what people meant when they talked about the Milky Way?

"Of course, it's nothing like the dark you used to get when I was a girl," said Japonica. "Now those were nights! You couldn't see your hand in front of your face."

Under the moonlight, Japonica was less human than ever. Her eyes glowed redder, and her skin deepened in color, not taking on the slight silver glow everything else had. She burned black and scarlet, and her beauty was as rich as the sky above.

Emily shivered and looked back to the stars. She didn't want to look away from them because, even with what she'd glimpsed from the corner of her eye, she was pretty sure there was something very wrong with the city. She had to know, though. Biting her lip, she looked down and took in all of London below.

Ah. Oh dear. Oh, dearie dear. That wasn't right at all.

CHAPTER 7

ave I gone back in time? I won't freak out if you tell me.
I watch *Doctor Who*."

"No, dear, you haven't. It is rather that time here hasn't gone anywhere."

"Oh, well that's much clearer, thank you."

It was London, but not her London. The city lay sprawled before her, still as huge as ever, but changed. The moon's silver illuminated it, but there were no streetlights, just a few tiny flickering gas lamps here and there. Hardly any of the buildings were lit up; in fact, most of the buildings just weren't there. There was no Shard, no Gherkin, no skyscrapers at all. Nothing taller than five or six stories, apart from the great old dome of St. Paul's. All the glass and steel had gone away, and the city had shrunk down to stone. She was standing on the roof of the post office building on St. Martin's Le Grand. The one that had been demolished in 1912. Also . . .

"Phwoar, it stinks."

"Ah! The reek of the Great Wen! It's bracing, isn't it? I'm told the sewers have improved a lot on your side."

"On my side of what? Please, Japonica, what's going on? I think I'm going bonkers."

She crammed a hand into her pocket to fish out a calming biscuit, and had to engage in a brief tug-of-war to do so. The Hog popped halfway out, still attached to the edge of the biscuit. Japonica bowed her head and bobbed a curtsy.

"Good evening, sir."

The Hog nodded back, fixed Emily with a grumpy stare, and went back in.

"That's it, I have gone bonkers." Emily sat down on the ledge and put her back to the wrong London. She stared at the nibbled edge of the biscuit for a moment, then shrugged and bit into it, anyway. Japonica sat beside her.

"I'm unfamiliar with the condition, but I'll try and explain."

She pursed her lips in thought then began.

"For the longest time, since we all emerged from the shadows and the forests, my people have lived alongside your people. The Night Folk and the Day Folk."

She patted Emily's shoulder.

"You're the Day Folk, dear."

"Yup, figured that."

"In the last century, magic started to run out. Your science and progress drove it from the world. We are creatures of magic as much as we are people of the night, and we need it to survive. Things grew desperate."

Her red eyes grew dark and bloody, and her face somber.

"We were on the brink of extinction until our protectors, the Older Powers, forged an alliance with your queen, Victoria. Our greatest sorcerers worked with your greatest scientists to make a unique device that combined magic and mechanics."

She got to her feet and held out a hand to pull Emily up, too.

"It was intended to make a place where it could be night forever, where magic could survive, and we could all be safe," said Japonica as she turned Emily around and pointed over her shoulder.

"There it is. The Great Working."

Her sharp, black-nailed finger pointed at Big Ben where it sat in the distance by the river. Big Ben, which Emily had seen every day, and heard every night, her whole life. Big Ben, which now, instead of being the comforting old clock tower, was a blazing pillar of light, wreathed in an emerald glow that started from the clock faces, and spiraled down in a glowing helter-skelter of fog. It showed midnight and burned in the darkness, and remained as blots in her eyes after she turned away.

"It first struck midnight in 1859, and, for us, that night never ended. The Great Working created the Midnight Hour, a frozen moment in time to be our sanctuary. All of the Night Folk and all of the remaining magic left the Daylight realm forever, and came here. Here where it is always pitch dark, always full moon, and always, always, midnight."

"Wow," said Emily, and meant it. "So, we're in 1859?"

"Effectively. We are in a frozen moment between the chimes of the clock that, on this side, will never tick or ring again. We are an unmoving island, whilst outside, in your world, the river of time flows on willy-nilly."

Emily tried to wrap her head around it all.

"So, all the night . . . people are in here? Is everyone . . . y'know, like you?" She gestured at Japonica's eyes and teeth.

"Ha! Is every one of your people like you?" Japonica mimicked her gesture and smiled her fangy, humorless smile. "No, we are all different, as you are. There are many different denizens of the Midnight Hour, but we are all, as one, the Night Folk."

"So, what are you?"

Japonica's eyes widened, and her pointed teeth crept out. Had they just gotten longer?

"Emily, I have to tell you it is considered dreadfully ill-mannered to ask that question. People's heritage is entirely their own business."

Emily gulped.

"I'm sorry."

"You were not to know, but it might be good to remember."

She smiled, teeth smaller again now.

"What I AM is Japonica Rhowse, friend of your father, and thus your friend, too."

She held her hand out and Emily shook it. It was still as cold as snowmelt, but Emily was warmer for shaking it.

"Now, we don't have long, so tell me what in Hecate's name are you doing here alone, and why did Alan recklessly desert his post?"

Emily told her everything. Japonica was a good listener. Her eyes glowed brighter at the exciting bits, but it seemed unwise to point that out. She nodded when Emily told her about the key turning in the door when she heard the bongs.

"Ah yes, that's all part of the Great Working, you see."

"What is?"

"You can only gain access to our Midnight Hour at exactly twelve, during the sound of the great bell's chimes. Even then, you need a door that exists both here and out there, and, oft-times, a key." Japonica's black-taloned (Emily had admitted to herself that's what they were) hand patted her leg.

"Lucky you had your father's spare! Clever of him to leave it."

"He didn't. I swiped it. It might have been cleverer of him to have mentioned any of this in the first place or left some actual instructions." She stamped her foot. "Why does he have a key? What's he got to do with all this?"

"I'm sorry, I thought we'd covered that. Your father works for the Night Post. He is, in fact, our Dangerous Deliveries Specialist."

Emily blew a raspberry as the laughter gushed out of her.

"Don't be daft. That's impossible."

Japonica nodded in agreement.

"Yes, his job rather is, but he's the very best we've got. A remarkable man. You must be proud."

"No, it's impossible that he's part of all this. He's my dad. He does . . . gardening, and . . ." There was some other stuff, but she couldn't put her finger on it, which just showed how boring it was.

Japonica gave her what Emily's mom would call "an old-fashioned look."

"You must have been born with great insight, to be so young and yet already know every corner of someone's heart."

Emily didn't reply, because she knew a burn when she heard one. After chewing on her knuckle, she stuttered out the thing she wasn't sure she wanted to know.

"So, is my dad . . . a monst–I mean, is he Night Folk, then? He does spend a lot of time in the shed, I guess."

"No, no, he's definitely Day Folk." Japonica laughed. Emily's tightly fisted hands unclenched.

"But how, why . . . ?"

"Your father works what we call the 'Night Shift.' He's one of the people from outside who come in to work in the Midnight Hour. It's rare but not unheard of. The Night Post is one of the remaining links between our worlds."

Emily's head was spinning. It was all too much to process. She was, if she was being honest, having as much trouble with her dad being "the best we've got" as the whole "secret world of monsters" thing.

"I . . ." Nope, still no working thoughts yet. Wait, there was the glimmering of one. "So, where is he? Where's my mom? Why did the horrid bear-thing mention her?"

Japonica's eyes flared a deeper crimson.

"I don't know, but the manifestation of the Bear in your world is a sign all is far from well." Japonica shook her head. "You say he only changed after he removed the umbrella?"

"Yes, that freaky little umbrella."

"It's a Night Shade, a tiny bit of midnight magic, charmed

into cloth. Underneath its shade, you are still within our Midnight. It's the only way magic can work in your world now."

"But he turned into a bear when he put it down!"

"He *is* a bear, dear. The magic lets him use his power to look human." She pursed her lips in worry. "The only people who should have Night Shades are the Post and the Watch for occasional missions in the Daylight realm. They're frightfully handy for deliveries, you know."

The steady flow of brain-exploding new things was hammering at her. When she was little, a wave had knocked her over at the seaside, and every time she'd tried to get up, the next wave had knocked her down again. This was worse. Her mom had come and picked her up back then. Who was going to help this time?

"I–I don't know what to do."

Japonica leaned in close.

"Your father did say one thing when he was here. I didn't mention it to the Postmaster because of the whole desertion thing."

"What?" Emily just about avoided screaming.

"He said only that he had to go to the Library and ask about the origins of a letter." Japonica held Emily's gaze with glowing red eyes as if she'd just shared an important secret.

"The library? For a letter?"

"Yes, I know. Something very unusual is going on. I think that's the best place for you to start."

"But, Japonica, look—" A terrible trumpeting noise cut over her. It was the megaphone again, its roar rattling and clattering out of the roof door. The noise of running feet on the stairs far below came with it.

Japonica leapt up.

"I'm afraid you must go now. I'd better get downstairs before he falls to pieces again." She grimaced. "It took ages to sew him back up last time."

"No, no, no!" said Emily, "I've got so many questions."

Japonica took her by the arm and did a brisk march across the roof to the far corner. "There's simply no time. The Night Watch are already here, and they'll kick you straight back into the Daylight realm, or worse."

In the corner was a set of steps up and over the roof ledge and onto a precarious metal stairway that ran down the outside of the building. Japonica urged her onto it. The noise from the stairwell was getting closer.

"Now, I'll go and tell them you ran off in a different direction, and that should buy you some time."

"But what am I supposed to do?"

"Go to the Library, and seek counsel there."

"*What* flippin' library?"

"Why, *the* Library, of course. Ask anyone."

Japonica was already walking toward the door, talking over her shoulder as she did.

"Actually, maybe not anyone." The pointy-toothed frown again. "A number of people here *really* didn't want to come into the Hour. They harbor grave ill-feeling toward the Day Folk."

Japonica ducked into the low, square doorway.

"Avoid dark alleys, the Night Watch, and the Hungry Dead. Don't make a bargain with Older Powers, and don't ever, ever trust a Pooka. Write to me here as soon as you know anything."

She disappeared into the dark, with only a red-eyed glint.

"Please, Japonica, you can't just leave me," Emily begged. From the darkness came shouted words.

"You're your father's daughter, you'll be fine!"

And then Emily was alone at midnight under the full moon.

CHAPTER 8

Emily clanged and jangled her way down the fire escape, then ran off down the grubby street at the bottom. She passed an old church, then St. Paul's loomed ahead of her on the right. That meant . . . got it! She was back on Foster Lane again. There was no longer a coffee shop or an office block in sight, and it wasn't quiet and empty anymore. In this London it was lined with low-slung buildings of wood and stone, cobbled streets filthy with mud, and a seething chaos of people and noise that made the Night Post's loading bay seem an oasis of calm.

If she'd had to guess, she would have said a London without cars or normal humans would be quiet but it was anything but. Midnight London roared. The main road on

Cheapside and the pavements around it were flooded with a raging torrent of people and traffic. Between the clatter of hooves, the crunchy grind of metal-banded wheels on cobbles, and the constant buzz, screech, chitter, and roar of the crowd, the noise was deafening.

The crowd was made up of the strangest people. They must have come from under beds and out of mirrors, up from caves and down from attics, all out of the darkness and into the moonlight. They were the Night Folk, and this was their world. They dressed as Victorians, but ranged from tiny to huge, from passing-for-human to not human at all. Grumpy-faced bearded men no higher than her knee, carrying big baskets of washing, weaving in between the legs of striding ogres with jutting tusks, prancing centaurs, and glowing specters dragging their chains. Among them people in smart suits with silver-headed walking canes, who she'd have taken for human if it hadn't been for the glimpse of a fang, or a reddened eye. They strolled alongside the walking rockfalls that were massive, trudging trolls, merfolk all covered in seaweed and ponging of fish, elbow-to-elbow with brisk, fur-faced wolf ladies and their packs of howling offspring. All around, everywhere she turned, were different sorts of Night Folk.

Her eyes and heart and head were overfull; the waterfall of images was a wonder, not terrifying, or at least not *just* terrifying. It was a feast, and for all the awfulness of what was happening to her, she knew this was something special she'd take with her for the rest of her life. Which might not be very long if any of the crowd got peckish . . .

Of all the things walking, sliding, and flapping past, the thing that most stuck out (after the epic monsterness, obvs) were the hats. Everybody had one. There was a dizzying variety of top hats, from toweringly tall ones in gleaming silk to battered and squashed things of thick brown card. There were bonnets, fancy floral numbers, and giant creations of silk and straw. The less well-off folk had boaters, bowlers, flat caps, scarves, and tied-on rags. The poorer you got, the flatter your hat. The variety was never-ending, and many of them had holes in to let out horns, or snakes, or eye-stalks, but apart from the urchins, every single person, as long as they had a head, had a hat on.

The middle of the road was a snarl of gryphon-drawn carriages, minotaur-pulled chariots, and a head-turning array of other types, including dog carts and weasel wagons for the smaller folk. They all rode and bounced across a cobbled road covered with such a deep layer of filth it made her gag from twenty yards away. Above it all was a constant flutter of bats, pigeons, glowing moths, small winged people (who had nowhere near enough clothes on for the weather), and the occasional long-winged, iridescent serpent, dancing in roiling knots that made Emily dizzy. Higher up was another layer of movement. At about the same height as the rooftops, larger things flew. There were actual *witches* on broomsticks, as well as an older witch in a flying armchair with, Emily could have sworn, a pot of tea on a table gliding beside her. In and out of the broomstick highway zoomed riders on big black bicycles, and the ring of a familiar bell drifted down. The Night Post were up there, too. She resisted the urge to wave but stood and gawped until someone walked straight into her.

"Blinkin' tourists! Some of us have to work here, you know!"

Before Emily could gasp an apology, the fur-faced thing had bristled past, and she'd been knocked into the path of another pedestrian, a top-hat-wearing confusion of fangs and eyeballs.

"I say!"

Emily had to spin and dodge to avoid him, finding herself hurled into the main flow of people on the street and right into the path of a pillar of stone that floated along with no apparent means of propulsion.

"Argh!"

"*%$@!"

She squeaked out of the way of getting crushed, got ping-ponged along the street, and ended up panting in a doorway, heart racing, as the crowd roared on past her. She squatted down, hugged her mom's jacket tightly around her, grabbed on to the necklace of pennies with one hand and ground them between her fingers as she wished to wake up, or just be anywhere but here. She muttered and rocked for a minute or two, then, as she pulled the coat tighter, an indignant squeak came from her pocket.

"Hoggins! I'm so sorry."

She eased her grip on the jacket, and teased him out of her pocket into her hand. She held him up before her and he wrinkled his nose, showing a tiny sharp tooth, but then softened and nuzzled the ball of her thumb with his nose.

"Hoggins, this is just . . . too much. What am I supposed to do?"

The Hog put his head on one side.

"I mean, Mom's missing, Dad's magic or something, and we're stuck in a bad horror movie. I am about to have a proper wobble." She fought down the tears, as she was not crying until she got out of here, no way. The Hog opened and closed his little mouth, then did it again, and nudged her with his nose. He might have been yawning but . . .

"Eat something? Good call."

Emily rummaged in her bag and pulled out a flattened sandwich. She bit into it, ignoring the nibble marks on the ham.

"Hoggins, you've got to stop eating my food. You'll turn into a porky-pine."

The sandwich, as always, made things better. She leaned back in the doorway, as the wall of legs, hooves, and tentacles went by, and held the Hog up to reconvene their meeting.

"Okay, we're stuck here, and we just need to get on with it, right? Whatever's going on with Mom, and Dad being . . . whatever he is . . . is *way* too much to think about right now. Let's just find them."

The Hog nodded, or maybe just twitched. It was difficult to tell. She fed him a leftover sliver of ham as she talked.

"But where are we supposed to go? Library? What flippin' libra—"

That rang a bell. The ridiculous idea of her mom being in a library at all and . . .

"The card!"

She rummaged in the pouch and pulled out the library card. It read:

BRITISH MUSEUM LIBRARY

MAEVE CONNOLLY

ASSISTANT LIBRARIAN TO KEEPER OF PRINTED BOOKS

And then a lot of funny words in what she guessed was Latin, with a very troubling date. So, a library card from 1859, and . . . nope, just going to think about it later. Or maybe never. The idea of her mom being an Assistant Librarian was even

more ridiculous than her dad being a magic postman but . . .
the British Museum! She knew where that was—somewhere in
Bloomsbury. That must be it.

"Hoggins, good chat, thanks. We totally have a plan."

The Hog had already fallen asleep on her lap, but she was
sure he was on board. She slid him back into her pocket with
tender care. For now, she just needed to get her bearings. If
St. Paul's was there, then the river was down there, and so
Bloomsbury must be . . . there! Got it. It was a pretty long
walk, though. Did the Victorians have the Tube? Or buses?
She still had some of the colorful old bank notes, as she was
pretty sure Oyster cards for the Tube hadn't been a thing in
the eighteenth century. Wait, that wasn't right, was it? She
always got that mixed up. Zero century was the first, so you
always had to add one. So, eighteen-something was actually
the nineteenth century. The eighteenth century had bigger
wigs and awesome dresses, and, she guessed as something
huge in a cloak stumped past her, fewer fangs.

Okay, head down, find a Tube or a bus stop, don't look
like a tourist. Or lunch. She braced herself, then ducked back
into the swell of people.

So, the Tube hadn't happened yet. Also, buses were pulled by
horses. Who knew? Great big tin-can things with stairs and

conductors and everything, but a set of horses (with worrying fangs) at the front, plodding away. They were crammed full of Night Folk, and even had people sitting on the roof. All the eyes and teeth were a bit much, she decided. The walk would do her good. It wasn't that far.

She'd gotten the rhythm of the streets more now. It was still a horrible press, but as long as you pressed back, and knew where you wanted to go, you made progress. The crowd kind of carried you along, but if you wavered, you just got swept away. It was going okay until she reached the first big road junction and had to stop. It was impossible to cross. The road was a solid mass of killer carriages, and full of the foulest dung. She watched how the Night Folk did it. People bunched up at the curb, then, when there were more of them than the traffic, they would force their way out, with some poor waif dressed in rags sent out first with a big broom to brush at least some of the horrid poo out of the way. It was well sketchy, and not on Emily's list of ideal weekend jobs.

She was just building up the courage to join the next suicide mission when she stopped dead in her tracks. Who was that? A tousle-haired boy, her age, and from her time, too, as she was pretty sure the Victorians didn't have jammies with robots on them. He stood swaying in his pajamas on the very edge of the curb, his eyes wide as he gazed all around. The crowd ignored him but, busy as it was, still left a distinct space around him. Emily forced her way over.

"Hey, are you all right?"

He didn't say a word, just stared in wonder at all the goings-on.

"Hey, are you okay? How did you get here?" She waved a hand in front of his eyes with no reaction, other than his growing grin.

"You're wasting your time, lad," said a voice of gravel from behind her. The voice came from behind a clanking contraption: a tall iron oven in a wheelbarrow, that had "Taters 'n' Toads for a penny" scratched out on it in chalk.

"He ain't proper here, is he? Blinkin' dreamlings. Gives ghosts a bad name, they do."

The boy *wasn't* properly here. He was transparent, a glimpse of the mayhem behind him visible through the robots fighting on his pajamas. He yawned, caught her eye, and there was a sudden thrill of connection. He *saw* her. He tipped his head to one side, pointed a finger at her, and opened his mouth to speak, but then slipped sideways through a fat unicorn, and vanished like a soap bubble popping.

"Whoa!"

"Best ignore 'em. Only encourages 'em."

"What are—"

His full-volume shout interrupted her: "TATERS! TATERS 'N' TOADS!" before he continued, "Y'what, son?"

She still hadn't seen his face, just the top of his hat moving behind the oven.

"What are they?"

"Dreamlings, int they. Dreamwalking over here. Blinkin' liberty if you ask me. They wanted clearing out with the rest of that daysie trash."

"But how—"

"TATERS! 'Ere, you're a bird, int ya? Why you got strides on, then? You ain't one of them daysies, are ya?"

"Certainly not!" said Emily in a deep voice. "I have to go now. Thank you, my good man." And with that she scooted, plunging along with the next road-crossing party. Behind her, the hat continued to yell from behind the oven.

"That's a liberty an' all! What's the world coming to?"

The crossings weren't getting any easier, but she was managing. She fumbled one of the old banknotes into the outstretched hand of the crossing sweeper as she got across the most recent one. From his wide eyes, abandoned broom, and immediate whooping departure up the road, she suspected she might have gotten the exchange rate a bit confused, but never mind. She broke off from the madness of the main road and headed up a quieter side street. The lack of noise was a relief, and she was pretty sure she was going the right way, too. For the first time since she'd gotten here, things were okay. She was doing it all by herself, and she wasn't that far away. Perhaps it was going to be all right after all?

"Ah ha! The wrong trousers!"

A firm hand took her by the shoulder and turned her around. Behind her was a tall and thin young man with glowing yellow eyes and pointy ears. He had clear brown skin and an ill-judged attempt at a mustache that wasn't doing him any favors. He wore a smart, navy-blue uniform with silver buttons, a shoulder cape and peaked cap, and had a truncheon hung from his black leather belt. He'd have been an imposing figure if he hadn't been so young. As it was, he might have been playing dress-up. He kept a hand on her shoulder and held his other hand right up to her face. In it was a mirror in a silver case.

"You match the Postmaster's description exactly. I'll have to ask you to look directly into this, please."

She didn't have much choice. The mirror moved and her reflection shifted and started to swirl. Her gaze was dragged into the whirlpool, and her head started to swim.

"Now you are under my command, and will do exactly as I say. I am Constable-in-Training Postlewhite of the Night Watch and you are under arrest for the crime of invading the sovereign borders of the Midnight Hour."

CHAPTER 9

The mirror glass whirled and roiled, then returned to her reflection. Emily started back.

"Oh!"

"Right, come along, then, miss, let's get you off to the lock-up."

The young man took his hand off her shoulder and gestured for her to walk ahead of him.

"Lock-up? No, I can't, I've got to get to the li–"

He spoke over her, slow and clear.

"Come with me. That is an order. You are under arrest."

"I'm trying to tell you, I can't. I've got to find my mom and dad."

His smooth brown brow wrinkled, and he looked at the compact silver mirror, now snapped closed in his hand.

"Wait, are you not feeling compelled to do what I say?"

"What? No. I'm feeling you're not listening, though."

He tapped the mirror and held it up to his ear.

"How strange." He glared at her. "You must not have done it properly. Here, look at this again."

He popped the mirror open and held it up in front of her face. It started to whirl, and Emily's furious reflection slid off into pattern and color before she batted his hand aside.

"Stop that! I'm trying to tell you something!"

He gnawed his lower lip. "Perhaps it's broken? Sarge will be furious." He took a step back, and started to pat his belt for something else, muttering under his breath. "Handbook says that in case of primary enchantment failure proceed to . . ."

He was an idiot. Why her? All of a sudden, there was a distinct whiff of something floral, the waft of perfume out of place in this stinking city.

"Just listen to me. You're a policeman, right?"

He looked up and straightened his hat, which had gone askew.

"I am an officer in good standing of the Night Watch, yes. As I said, you are under–"

"Arrest," Emily finished for him. "I know. But I haven't done anything, and I totally need a policeman to help me."

Constable-in-Training Postlewhite drew himself up and squared his shoulders.

"That's for me to decide and I'm afraid, miss, that you have broken a host of border agreements, not to mention your violations against public decency." He nodded at her trousers. "Hence, I am arresting you and taking you to the station to be processed with due, erm, process. Now . . ." And with this he drew his truncheon, which was banded with silver and had a pointy end. ". . . I must insist you come with me."

"Fine, fine. Whatever." She put her hands up. "Is there someone I can speak to there who's not an idiot?"

"Oh yes," he said, eyes alight with eagerness. "The Sarge, I mean, my sergeant is . . . wait." He pursed his lips like he'd tasted something sour. "There's no need to be like that. I'm just doing my job."

"Is your job to aid helpless people whose parents are missing and who've been chased by a giant bear?"

"Absolutely!" He raised his truncheon to what was doubtless the approved bear-defense posture. "Why, do you know someone?"

"YES! Me!"

"Oh. Are you sure?"

"Oh goodness, you're right, I'm all confused about my

parents BEING GONE, AND ALSO THE BEAR!" She was now shouting at the policeman with the pointy stick. Great. Good job, gob. The pointy stick and the young man had both taken a step back in the face of her wrath.

"Right, fair enough. Erm. Can you think where you last saw them?"

Emily ground her teeth before answering.

"I haven't lost them down the back of the couch. They've gone missing. In here."

She might as well have chucked a bucket of cold water on him. There was another gust of fragrance, this time more robust and herby. Sage?

"You mean there are more in your party?" The truncheon snapped back up to guard position. "How many? What are you planning?" His other hand groped for something inside his jacket.

Emily groaned with despair.

"For the love of . . . no. My dad works here, at the Night Post. He's on the, do you call it the Night Shift?"

The scrabbling hand pulled out a big silver whistle on a cord. It was halfway to his mouth when the mention of the Night Post sent him scrabbling back inside his jacket for a black leather-bound pad. He fumbled his truncheon and whistle between both hands as he opened the pad while trying not to take his gaze off Emily, going cross-eyed in the process.

"Night Post? Oh ho, this is the 'Day Folk post-deserter' you're on about, isn't it? The Postmaster has told me all about your lot." He stuck his chin out. "You don't fool me with your sob story!"

The triumphant accusation was interrupted by his dropping first pad then truncheon and having to struggle to pick them up. Emily let out a long and weary sigh.

"It's not a sob story, and my dad is not a deserter." She had no idea what her dad actually *was* anymore, but figured she'd work that out after she'd found him.

"You can tell it to the judge," said the young policeman in what he doubtless imagined were tough tones. He'd stowed all his things now and was advancing on her with a pair of silver manacles he'd produced from some inner pocket. "No more stories, you're coming with me."

"No, is not," said a horrible yet familiar growl of a voice. "Told her already, girl is mine."

From a darkened alley behind the policeman, stepped the Bear.

He'd abandoned the ridiculous umbrella and still looked more bear than human. The remnants of the tweed trousers hung in rags, and he was standing upright, but the huge furry torso and massive, clawed paws were all bear. His face was the worst thing of all, still with a glimpse of the man, but with a fanged snout sticking out of the black fur, and a great, lolling pink tongue that flapped as his teeth mangled his words. The same paralyzing wave of cold fear from before pinned Emily to the floor again. Her hand crept to the Hog, but he had rolled up tight into a prickly ball. She wished she could do the same.

"Knew I smelt daysie flesh." The Bear was talking to someone behind him, and a small gang of horrors trooped out of the dark. There were five of them, all smaller than the Bear but bigger than Emily. They had identical banged-up, stony-skinned faces, pointy ears, and jutting tusks, and they each wore a coarse brown three-piece suit and flat cap. They fanned out on either side of the Bear to fill the alley. With them was a tall, handsome man, a butterfly among drab moths. He was bone pale, with knife-edge cheekbones and slicked-back hair. He was wearing a red silk–lined opera cape over a well-cut black velvet suit, and sharp teeth poked out from beneath his top lip. He might as well have been carrying a sign that said, "Ask me anything about vampires."

"I don't know how you can smell anything over the reek of this riff-raff," said the vampire, gesturing languidly at the goblin henchmen. "I shall take over now, of course."

The Bear ignored him, and grinned at Emily.

"Good running, little rabbit. Nearly lost Bear outside. Lucky other door near." He sniffed, and licked his big teeth. "But running is over now. Easy to smell bad luck and paint. Easy to smell you." He sniffed once more and wrinkled his nose up in confusion. "Also smell flowers. Strange."

Constable-in-Training Postlewhite had been staring, mouth agape, at the new arrivals. At the Bear's last words, he flushed, then shook himself and stood as tall as he could before them.

"Gentlemen, I am an officer of the Night Watch, and you are interrupting an arrest. I shall have to ask you to disperse before I am forced to take measures."

There was a silence that dragged on as the Bear's gang stared at him and nudged one another, grinning. Emily had a surge of sympathetic embarrassment for the young policeman that overwhelmed her utter terror. Although not for long. An awful sound shattered the silence, like broken glass being rolled down the stairs in an iron barrel. It was the laughter of the Bear.

"A HUR A HURH HURHG HURHGH!"

His whole chest shook, and he slammed a paw against the wall to hold himself up. The wall cracked and brick dust trickled out where he had hit it. Around him, his tusked henchmen all cracked up, too. Even the vampire deigned to give a sardonic, toothy smile. Constable-in-Training Postlewhite's shoulders slumped. As the laughter continued he shrank down into himself, and stared at the floor.

"Ahurgh." The Bear quieted and wiped his streaming eyes

with a massive paw. "Agh, is good. Best joke Bear hear in last two century."

The Bear drew himself up, all humor gone from his voice. "So, you go now. Leave girl for us, and I not eat you today."

Behind the Bear, the hideous goblin quintuplets reached into their pockets and produced various sharp and heavy objects. The vampire slid away, lip curled from pointy teeth in distaste. The policeman trembled and took a step back. The street had emptied of other people, the wind of the Bear's laughter blowing them all away.

"GO!" roared the Bear at top volume, and the young man turned, his scared eyes locking on Emily's. He looked away, face crumpling, and Emily waited for him to sprint past her into the night. Instead, he turned back around, positioned himself in front of her, and raised his truncheon. A distinct scent of honeysuckle filled the air.

"No," he said.

There was a ripple of surprise from the gang, and the Bear's grin grew wide.

"No. Absolutely not," Constable-in-Training Postlewhite continued. "This is my prisoner and I have a sacred duty." As he spoke he was fumbling inside his jacket and produced the great big silver whistle. "Now, I suggest you run before my colleagues arrive."

He finished his sentence and jammed the whistle in his

mouth, and was just about to blow it when a huge paw swung in out of nowhere, smashed him in the shoulder, and knocked him all the way across the alley into the wall with a horrid crunch. The Bear crossed the space between himself and Emily before the policeman had even slid down the wall, and now stood right over her. There was a stench of sour fat and rotting meat. Across from her, Constable-in-Training Postlewhite fell to the floor without a sound and lay still.

"Now, girl. Nowhere to go."

"I was just about to leap into action there," said the vampire as he appeared by the side of the Bear. He moved cat-quick and twice as silent, a dancer next to the Bear's lumbering mass. He sniffed with disgust as he glanced down at the crumpled policeman. "Not particularly subtle, eh? Now, it's best if I step in, don't you think? Her ladyship did send me especially."

The Bear turned with a snarl.

"Bear find. Bear bring back."

"As you say, dear chap, as you say." The vampire glided back out of paw range. The Bear leaned in, his huge fanged maw right by Emily's cheek, and snorted. The freezing fear became worse and worse, and there was a chance her heart might stop from it.

"Smells like the mother."

Who'd have guessed it was possible to go from being about to poo yourself with terror to a white-hot anger?

"What have you done with my MOM?!" she screamed right in the Bear's ear, who reared back away from the unexpected noise. He reached to grab her, but as he did, there was a weird liquid sensation in her chest and neck, and she slipped out from under his paw. Half a second later, she was on the other side of the alley from him, while he was still swinging at the empty space where she'd been.

"What?" she gasped.

All eyes in the alley were still staring at the Bear, but now flicked across to her.

"Crikey!" said the vampire.

"Get her!" roared the Bear.

"Calm down, old chap," said the vampire as he flowed toward Emily, cape flicking out behind him. "I am the ultimate predator of the night. She's not going anywhere." He cocked his head. "I say, can you hear a horse?"

As he spoke, a black stallion cantered around the corner. It was a magnificent beast, black as sin all over, with a splash of pure white in the top of its mane, and glowing red eyes. It skidded, then charged at full speed, straight over the vampire, crushing him into the cobblestones without even a squeak.

CHAPTER 10

The horse skidded to a halt in the midst of the gang, hooves still on the flattened and twitching vampire. The Bear had just opened his snout to say something when the horse wheeled neatly around and kicked him so hard with its back hooves that he flew into the air before crashing into the wall with a meaty thump. Before anyone could do more than gasp, the horse was in among the goblins.

It whinnied a high-pitched shriek, reared up on its hind legs and crashed down among them, front legs flailing. The horse was a whirlwind of teeth and lashing hooves, bucking and kicking and spinning and biting as the goblins screamed and tried to get out from under the sudden storm. The Bear lay against the wall, curled on his side, paws clutched to his vast stomach as he tried to breathe. All he could squeeze out were tiny little wheezing noises, drool falling from his slack jaws.

Emily hadn't moved an inch. The stallion stared straight at her from inside the cloud of dust and screaming henchmen, lips pulled back from huge teeth in an unholy grin. In an ever-so-human gesture, it flicked its head to the right. She gawped, and it did it again—it was a clear, "go on, get out of here" type of head movement. The madness of it jolted her into action. She turned to run and had gone three paces before she let out a hiss, and turned back to where Constable-in-Training Postlewhite lay in a crumpled heap. She grabbed him by the collar and shook him. He stirred with a moan.

"Come *on*, we have to go."

"I . . . what? Where?" He blinked and sat up, in a billowing cloud of scent. It *was* coming from him. Had he smashed a bottle of perfume in the fall or something?

"Come on! We have to go now!"

She yanked him to his feet and he wobbled, but the light was returning to his yellow eyes. He started to flail at his belt for his missing truncheon.

"I must alert the Watch and make arrests. My duty . . ."

"I don't care if it's your duty to do the moonwalk! They're going to eat us if we stay."

The stallion still whirled and shrieked, but it was slowing, all streaked with sweat and blood. (Not that any of the blood was its own. It was a bad day to be a goblin.) On the other side of the alley, the Bear had rolled onto his front and was trying to get up. He was growling the low, bubbling noise of a monster truck. The stallion glared at Emily with its bright-red eyes and gave a high-pitched whinny.

"Right, I'm off!" she snapped at the policeman and turned to go. "Enjoy being finger food."

"I'm coming, I'm coming."

Half dragging, half carrying the wobbly young man, she stumbled for the nearest alley mouth. They threw themselves into the darkness and he managed a staggering run alongside her. They'd just built up to a jogging pace, when a horrific roar of rage echoed around them, a ripping, deep-throated chainsaw of a noise. The Bear had gotten his breath back. Without either of them speaking, they started to sprint, skating from cobblestone to cobblestone and careering off walls as they hurtled away, the roar echoing behind them through the dark.

An endless time later, they sagged against a wall in a dank backstreet, heaving for air. Emily hadn't run so much in years (not since she'd managed to get her mom to absentmindedly sign a "no games ever" note, anyway), and was not enjoying having to do it for the third time in a day. She leaned forward, hands on her knees, the necklace of bad pennies dangling out of her T-shirt with beads of sweat dripping off them. She sucked in the cold night air and concentrated on not throwing up.

"Thank you for helping me to escape. That was very honorable." The young policeman was out of breath but not as beet red and panting as Emily was. "I think under the circumstances, we should be properly introduced. I'm Tarquin. Constable-in-Training Tarquin Postlewhite."

"Emily Featherhaugh, and s'okay," she said in between gasps. "You tried to stand up for me. That was brave."

He smiled and did what she suspected was his best brave face. It didn't do his excuse for a mustache any favors.

"Merely my duty, Miss Featherhaugh."

"If utterly stupid."

He deflated.

"Oh."

"What was all that about? Do you have police attack horses or something?"

"No, that was a Pooka. I've never seen one before, but the red eyes . . ." He shook his head in wonder. "They're beasts of ill-omen—rare and powerful, and terribly unlucky."

"Unlucky for that bloke it jumped up and down on, anyway," said Emily.

"Yes, but fortuitous for us. That's unusual in itself." He

winced as he rubbed his already bruising neck and shoulder. "You certainly weren't making it up about the Bear."

"I told you!"

"He's formidable. I think he might be an Ancient Beast." Tarquin smiled at her. "Don't worry, I'll be sure to mention it in mitigation to my sergeant when I hand you in."

"What?"

He inched back from Emily, but composed himself.

"I've no choice. Your assistance was appreciated, although I'm sure I'd have managed . . ."

She was too out of breath to do any more than growl at him.

"But that was a direct attack on the Watch by denizens of the Hour. It hasn't happened in years. So you're a subject of interest in two separate investigations now and will have to come with me."

He drew himself up, straightened his muddy cape, and inflated back to the same self-important muppet he'd been when they first met.

"Oh my god, you're a total . . . wait, what do you mean, two?"

"Well yes, first we need to find out how on earth you got in. That should be impossible." He counted off on his fingers. "And secondly, what these villains wanted with you. If you're not in league with them. Which . . ." He raised a hand to stop her shouting. ". . . I'll grant it didn't look as if you were. But it's all become very serious and we need to take it to a higher authority."

Was she going to erupt or just spontaneously combust? Tricky decision. Instead, she spoke her next words with great care, as if speaking to a complete idiot. Which, in fact, she was.

"I got in with a key. This key." She opened her bag and pulled it out, and waved it, show-and-tell style. "It belongs to my dad. He works for the Night Post." She waved the badge in the wallet. "And I don't know why that bear is chasing me, but I have to get to the library to find out why my dad was going there."

Constable-in-Training Postlewhite narrowed his eyes.

"The Library?"

"Yes, the library. My mom might have worked there, I think. I've got her stupid library card." She held it up. "I've got to find out what's happened. Mom's gone missing and my dad hasn't come back, either, and it's something to do with that horrible bear. If we could just go there on the way or something then . . ."

She stopped talking. Constable-in-Training Postlewhite was staring at the library card she'd held up. He took it from her and studied it with a low whistle.

"Crikey. This is your mother's, you say?"

"Yes."

"She has a Library card?"

"Yeees." Perhaps he'd banged his head harder than she'd thought when he hit the wall?

"Well, I'll be."

"All right. Sarcasm's *my* job."

Tarquin's eyes glowed honey-bright.

"No, you don't understand. The bestowing of a Library card is a sacred trust conferred on few."

"Errrm?"

"What exactly did your father say about the Library?"

Whenever he mentioned the words "the library," he was adding an extra level of gravity to the way he said it. Like, the *Titanic*, or, the War.

"The nice lady at the Night Post said that he had to go to the library to check out where a letter had come from."

Which, when she said it aloud, sounded a bit daft. Why leave a perfectly good post office to go to the library if you were researching a letter?

Tarquin paced away, staring at the card.

"Hrrrrrrrmmmmm."

"Seriously, what's the big deal?" said Emily.

He handed it back to her.

"I should take you back to the station, but if the Library is involved, then you should go there first."

"Great!" Emily bounced up. "What's the problem, then?"

"Well." He wrung his hands together, his face creased with worry. Despite the uniform, he must have been only a few years older than her. "There's an order here. The Dead run everything night-to-night, like the Watch and the post, but the—"

"Wait, who's dead?"

"You know, the *Dead*. Hungry Dead? Angry Dead? All the other types? No?"

Emily shook her head. "Wait, so all the dead here are like . . . alive?" she said.

"Don't be ridiculous. They don't let just *anyone* come back. That'd be madness. Only the important people . . ."

He was pacing again now.

"But the most important things in the Midnight Hour are the forces that created it and saved us all, the Older Powers. The Library is among their number."

"A library?"

"*The* Library. We'd be going straight to the top." His face was mournful at the prospect.

"Brilliant. That's just what I want."

"My father has strong views on not being noticed by people at the top," Tarquin said.

"You can stay outside, then."

"I suppose so." He drew himself back up. "I've heard some strange stuff about the Library. Very strange indeed."

How strange did something need to be over here, before people would actually mention it?

"And the Bear was in your world?"

His face was a mask of very grown-up concern (which, Emily hadn't the heart to tell him, made his mustache look even sillier).

"That shouldn't even be possible. Most denizens are strictly forbidden to leave the Midnight Hour for their own good. The Daylight realm is dangerous."

He turned and gave her what she was coming to recognize as his "official police look." She was pretty sure he must have copied it off of someone.

"He took a terrible risk. Why on earth are they after you?"

"I have no idea. He just keeps on sniffing me down. Says I smell like bad luck—"

Emily stopped dead in the middle of the footbridge they were walking over, and clutched at her necklace.

"Oh god, he's just going to sniff me down again, isn't he? I need to jump in a sewer or something."

She spun on her heels. He could already be creeping up on them! She leaned out over the edge of the bridge; maybe the rivulet of black water below might be stinky enough to cover her smell? A green-blotched troll face peered back up from under the bridge and made a very rude gesture at her. Tarquin put his hand on her arm before she could hurl herself in.

"Just wait, please."

He checked all around to see if anyone was watching, then turned back to her, his cheeks flushing with color. The embarrassment changed to concentration and his tongue crept out of the corner of his mouth as he held out a hand toward Emily. He drew his hand slowly around her from head to toes, as if marking her outline in chalk. As he did, the air was suffused with the rich, cloying odor of violets. Emily coughed. From within her pocket came a small but distinct sneeze.

"Whoa! You made me smell of old-lady sweets! How did you do that?"

Tarquin's face tightened.

"I don't want to talk about it. Come along."

"Oh, come on, you can't just cover me in magic perfume then say nothing." She bounced along at his side. "That was amazing!"

She was walking backward in front of him now.

"Can you do other smells? Can you do Chanel No. 5? You could have your own counter at Harrods and make a fortune!"

"Please, please stop talking."

"But how did you do that? What are y–" She stopped, in

a hurry, as he looked up to glare at her. "No, sorry, forget I said that. I know it's rude."

Tarquin heaved a sigh.

"No, it's all right. I'm ghûl."

"A ghoul?"

"No, ghûl."

"Guhool." She rounded her lips and tried to speak from the back of her throat like he was.

"Almost. Close enough, in fact. My family are ghûl, and this exact type of misunderstanding is the problem. Ghouls," and he enunciated it so the difference was obvious, "eat the dead. Very prestigious. My family eat . . . other things."

He gave a small twisted smile.

"What exactly?"

"Nothing. You wouldn't understand." He was waving his hands around, grasping for an explanation. "There are just . . . look, people have different backgrounds and are treated differently."

"Yeah, we have that, too."

"Not like here. You must never mention I did this."

"But the smelly thing is so cool!"

His brow creased.

"Does that mean good?"

"Yup."

"Well, it's not. If I could eat the dead and take their power, that would be . . . whatever you just said. But I eat . . . other things, and smell nice. Very much not cold."

"Oh."

He stopped and leaned against a lamppost. Above his head, giant moths battered against the glass with heavy thumps, and his eyes burned the same color as the tip of the gas flame.

"Honestly, I think the recruiting sergeant wrote the wrong type of 'ghoul' down when I applied to join the Watch. I don't know how, they sound totally different."

"Uh-huh."

"I'm not sure I'd have the job if they knew," he said to himself, then stopped. "Hecate, why am I telling you this?"

"Because I am famed as a very good listener."

"Truly?"

"No, not at all. But it was interesting."

He drew himself up to his full height, pulled his cape down with a brisk tug, and gave her the policeman look.

"I put you on your honor that, having done this to protect you, it will not be mentioned again."

"I won't tell anyone, okay?"

His rigid posture relaxed.

"Thank you. Come along, then, we aren't far away now."

"As long as you de-arrest me."

"WHAT?"

"Come on, Violet. You know it makes sense."

CHAPTER 11

B y the time they'd rounded the final corner, Tarquin was keeping a steady ten, deeply irritated paces in front of Emily. Even here, in another magical world, her gob annoyed people. It was a superpower. As they walked on in silence, the dark streets snapped into place as a picture she recognized.

"Wait, I've been here before. We're right by the museum, yeah?"

Tarquin nodded in a frosty manner but said nothing, and carried on around the corner. She found him standing outside an open gate in a stone wall. Beyond it was a graveled courtyard, and then stone steps leading up to a vast, columned portico at the front of the building. It was as much a Greek temple as a museum. Tarquin stared at it without saying anything.

"Are you still sulking?"

"I am an officer of the Night Watch. I do not sulk. I am just . . ." He looked away from the doors. "I am just . . ."

"Wait, are you scared?" Seeing him worry was a . . . worry, but it made him more human. Apart from the golden eyes and pointy ears, anyway.

"No! Just . . . cautious. She is an enigma."

"Who?"

"The Library."

"Eh?"

He ignored her, squared his shoulders, and started toward the stairs. She hustled along behind him, definitely not scared, either. Definitely . . .

He heaved open a great metal-bound door and walked into the tall atrium, striding across the marble floor, and she hurried to keep up. The museum entrance was vast and quiet, and ringed with glinting things in cases. In the middle was a tall wooden rostrum, with a goat-man seated behind it. He wore a black vest over a pristine white shirt, with a thin black necktie, but had the head, horns, and creepy horizontal pupils of a goat. He was smoking a thin black cigarillo. It was hanging out of the corner of his long muzzle, and dangling perilously close to his splendid chin-beard. Emily edged a bit to the side, but the rostrum curved too far around. She'd have bet five quid he had hooves.

"Good evening, we're here to see the Library," said Tarquin.

The goat-man picked up a pair of half-moon spectacles from where they dangled at the end of a chain around his neck and brought them to his eyes. They had a huge bridge in the middle to go over his broad nose. Emily was pretty sure he only put them on just so he could look down over them.

"I see. I'm afraid all usage of the reading room must be cleared with the Keeper of Printed Books." As he spoke, a whiff of tobacco and cut grass drifted from him. "I see no note about an appointment here . . . sir."

There had been a good second before that "sir." He inspected a blank piece of paper in front of him, then looked back up with a thin smile. At no point did he look at Emily. She recognized his type straight away, goat face or not.

Tarquin was unfazed.

"I'm afraid you've misunderstood me . . . sir." He held his hand out to Emily without looking at her. "Miss Featherhaugh, the card please."

Emily was impressed at this coolness, although less so at the "finger-snapping-at-assistant" mode he had fallen into. She had a quick scrabble in her bag and then, stepping straight past Tarquin's outstretched hand, slapped the library card on the counter.

"We're here to see THE LIBRARY," she said with extra emphasis. "My good man," she added, just in case it wasn't clear she was patronizing him.

The goat-man took one look at the card and blanched. Well, she was sure he had, but it was hard to tell with the hairy face and all. What he did do was push his stool back with a nasty squeaking noise, to be farther away from the card and them.

"You'll . . . you'll need to go straight ahead. Down the corridor, big green door, go straight into the reading room." He was looking anywhere but directly at them. Emily leaned in and grabbed the card back. She caught Tarquin's eye and shared a quick conspiratorial smile.

"Well, thank you, you've been EVER so helpful." Quick count to three. "Sir."

They bustled off down the corridor goat-man had pointed to. As they passed the desk, Emily glanced back.

"Ha, knew it! Goat feet!"

They entered the reading room, and Emily let out an involuntary, "Whoa!" The room was circular and huge, lined with books right up to where the incredible dome of the ceiling arched off above them, all blue, cream, and gold. Moonlight spilled in through the central skylight and the many slanted windows, setting it all aglow. Emily spun around and around as they walked, mouth open at the mass of leather bindings of every color that lined the shelves. From the walls in were aisle after aisle of concentric shelves, curved to match the walls, and looking like a labyrinth from above. The open center of the room was filled with chairs and reading desks, all spread with books. It was a little bit of heaven, although there was no obvious sign of a kettle or biscuit jar, which was an important part of any reading experience in her opinion.

The shelved walls around them were filled with a mass of books, papers, and scrolls, and the air with a deep, musty perfume of ancient dust and ink. As the warm glow of their little victory over the goat faded, she thumbed the library card in her pocket. What had the wide-nosed git been so chicken of? Where exactly were they going? She turned to ask Tarquin, but his clenched teeth and hesitant steps gave away that he was more scared than the goat had been. Great. A little chill started to spread up her spine, too, and her hand moved to the bad pennies. She stroked them, letting her finger graze each coin, the patterns on them rough under her fingers, and the chill receded.

"So, this is what, a secret base or something, right?"

"What?"

"This whole 'the Library is an Older Power and very important' bit. This is their secret base or something, yeah?"

He stopped, eyes narrowed.

"Their base? No, this is where all the books are. Where else would you find the Library?"

Way down a long, curved aisle lined with red leather-bound folios, there was a flicker of movement. Tarquin squinted into the shadows thrown by the shelves, his yellow eyes flaring into liquid gold, and grabbed her arm.

"There she is."

"Who?"

"The Library, of course." He squeezed her arm harder. Too hard, in fact. Was his mustache trembling? "Now, we must approach quietly and respectfully. She may be . . . unusual to deal with."

"Wait, you mean the Library is a person?"

"I don't think I could have been any clearer, could I? Come on." He started to edge toward the movement at the end of the aisle.

Emily stood stock-still and glared at his back, grinding her teeth. Was throwing a book at his head an arrestable offence?

As they moved closer, the movement resolved itself into a form. At the end of the row of shelves stood a lanky beanpole of a woman, with long white hair and olive skin. She wore a long, tattered white drapery of silk and lace that might just have been the remains of a wedding dress, with one silk slipper on and one bare foot. She was holding one of the huge books one-handed, as if it weighed no more than a paperback. She was talking, under her breath but with great intensity, perhaps reading aloud. She wasn't looking at the book, though.

Tarquin cleared his throat, and without glancing up, she moved away from them around the curve in the shelving, placing the book down, still open, as she did. Emily wouldn't have sworn to it, but she might have floated off rather than walked. Emily and Tarquin looked at each other with wide eyes, raised open hands in a shrug, and headed after her. As they picked up their pace, there were other open books, discarded here and there, on the floor and shelves, all left half-read and abandoned, a trail of literary breadcrumbs. As they rounded the curve, at the far end of the aisle was the Library, as tall as the tallest shelves, in the middle of a snowdrift of books stacked in haphazard piles around her. She was holding a small green book, still muttering, and not looking back at them. Yup, definitely floating.

"I don't know what to do," Tarquin said. "The only thing I've ever heard about her is that you mustn't disturb her when she's reading."

"What? So, we could die of old age whilst the hovering book hoover ignores us and my mom and dad stay lost?"

Emily slid from fear into anger like pulling on a pair of comfy old slippers. "Stuff that."

She cupped her hands into a cone and shouted through them, even as Tarquin tried to grab at her to stop her.

"OI! BOOKFACE! WE WANT TO TALK TO YOU!"

The Library stopped in mid-float and spun toward them with a dancer's grace. There was a still, silent moment, then her eyes flashed, and she flew toward them at great speed, gabbling in tongues. They both screamed and clutched at each other as she crossed the distance in a flash. She stopped an inch from them, her long-nosed face full of outrage, her eyes a terrible roiling mix of black and white, like ink in water. An electric shock of fright shot up Emily's spine as the Library's long white hair slicked out around her and brushed Emily's face. The ragged white dress billowed, floating as if the Library was underwater, and she screeched in a hundred languages, right in their faces. Not one word in ten made sense but snatches of phrases came through as Emily pressed herself back against the shelves.

"Thou hadst been better have been born a dog, than answer my waked wrath!"

"Rage—Goddess, sing the wrath of Peleus's son Achilles, and its devastation."

"Give me yourself and your hatred; give me yourself and that pretty rage."

There was no end to it. Tarquin was statue-rigid and had closed his eyes. Brilliant. Emily inched a hand into her pocket and pulled out the library card from under a quivering Hog, and then thrust it in front of those alien eyes.

"I'M HERE BECAUSE OF MY MOM AND DAD!"

The noise stopped. Emily had closed her eyes as she'd shouted, and when she opened them the Library had moved back a couple of yards and was standing (well, hovering) in perfect stillness, face turned up to the dim lighting above. Her haunting eyes were shut, her whole face pulled tight, and her head was moving in spasms as if some vast internal battle was being fought. Her hands were clenched into fists, tawny knuckles white with effort. She stayed that way for several seconds, long enough for Emily and Tarquin to exchange bewildered glances, then she breathed out, unclenched her hands, and opened her eyes again. She still stared at the light above, but her eyes were back to normal, not the nightmare pools they had been.

"Are you here?" The Library's voice was dry and dusty, and rattled in her throat. She still wasn't looking at them.

"Erm, yep, pretty sure we are. Deffo."

"Good. So many words, over so much time. Sometimes it's hard to know which are happening right now."

"Erm, yeah, I totally understand," said Emily, who didn't. "My mom never knows what day it is, either."

The Library spun in the air to face them and her one bare foot and one slippered foot touched the floor. All of a sudden, she was more vivid than she had been before, more present, as if she'd come into focus. She looked them both up and down without smiling.

"Yes, let us talk of your mother, Emily Featherhaugh."

CHAPTER 12

How do you know my name?”

"If it is written of by man, then it is part of me. There is little new writing in the Midnight Hour, but some of it has concerned you." She looked at Emily, and a flicker of a smile passed across her lips. "Also, you have your mother's card, and mouth it would seem. The resemblance is striking."

"You *do* know my mom!" She'd already known they were connected but hearing it direct from the giant floaty book lady was just downright odd.

"Where is she? Where's my dad? He was coming here."

With a sniff of policing in the air, Tarquin regained the power of speech.

"Great Lady, what has gone on here? The boundaries of the Midnight Hour have been breached, we've been attacked by the Hungry Dead and an Ancient Beast, and I don't know what the Sarge is going to say."

The Library turned a hard stare on him.

"Well, I don't. He's very shirty." He flushed, coughed, then looked at his shoes. The Library continued as if he hadn't spoken.

"Another force is at play. She threatens us all."

Emily's eye began to twitch.

"What? I seriously need you to explain what is going on, or I'm going to . . . to . . . fold all your pages over, and . . . move all your bookmarks, or something."

The Library raised one thick eyebrow at her.

"Listen, then," said the Library and her voice was different now, harsher, as dried out as the old papers around them. "We were three—"

"Wait," Emily interrupted. "Are you quoting again?" It was her turn to receive an arch look from the Library, and she, too, found her shoes to be fascinating straight afterward.

"We were three sisters, first of the Night Folk, sprung from your dreaming minds at the dawn of humanity. I am Language, the youngest. My sister Art was before me, daubed on cave walls in ochre and blood. But before us both was our oldest sister, Music. She was born with the first stamp of feet, and clatter of sticks, with the whistle of the wind and the cry of the wolf."

The Library's hands swayed at her sides as she spoke, and her hair started to stir again. If she was starting at the dawn of time, how long was this story going to take?

"Eons later, facing the death of magic, we forged an agreement with your queen, Victoria, to make the Great Working. We would leave your world forever to preserve the magic and save our people."

Emily sneaked a glance at Tarquin. He was looking down and his eyes were suspiciously moist-looking. What had upset him?

"Our oldest sister, known as the Nocturne in this age, did not agree. She is wildness and raw beauty and would not be contained."

The Library's face rippled with shadows and was terrible, sad, and majestic all in one. In that moment, she was difficult to watch.

"The Nocturne lured many of the Angry Dead to her cause and would have warred on your world instead. I love her but . . . could not allow it. There was a terrible battle. Art and many others were lost to our sister's rage but we won and left forever."

"What's *any of this* got to do with my *mom*?" Emily said.

"Your mother was the hero of that battle. She deprived

the Nocturne of a terrible weapon. We couldn't have won without her."

"What? When? Do you mean long-ago times?" said Emily. "Why was my mom in a battle?" She didn't quite shriek, but there was a definite raising of voice as she went on. Tarquin shot her a warning look she ignored.

"Your mother has been our bravest defender since before we entered the Midnight Hour, its greatest protector once we did."

"WHAT?!" said Emily.

"So, she *was* a Librarian?" gasped Tarquin at the same time.

The Library inclined her head in a nod.

"Uh?" said Emily

"Very important," gabbled Tarquin out of the side of his mouth. "Secret missions to protect the Midnight Hour."

Emily closed her eyes. She definitely had a headache coming on.

"Yes, a loyal servant of Midnight," said the Library. She paused and twitched her head around, as if hearing something behind her. The corners of her eyes were filling with blackness again. She turned back to them, and her expression was different: wistful, and melancholy. *"Midnight. We have heard the chimes at midnight, Master Shallow."*

"Whoa there!" said Emily. "Back in the room. We're here!"

The Library shook her head as if trying to get water out of her ears, and the black in her eyes receded.

"I-it is . . . difficult for me since the creation of the Great Working. I am not as I was."

The Library's face was bleak as she said this and, without thinking, Emily reached out and patted her on the arm. Tarquin coughed a choking noise and his eyes bulged.

"Are you okay? Are you . . . hearing voices?" said Emily. That was not a question she had expected she was going to have to ask anyone this week. The Library came close to another smile.

"I *am* voices, Emily Featherhaugh. I come from words and thus all your voices are in me." She waved her hand to indicate every shelf in the reading room. "But now, shut off from your world, without new words from you, I fade into my memories. It was the sacrifice that had to be made to save the Night Folk."

For once, Emily didn't know what to say. The Library gathered herself and continued.

"We stopped the Nocturne back then, but now she has re-emerged, still strong, while I am reduced to a shadow of my former power. I do not know why my sister has not faded, but she plots in my weakness." The Library looked straight at Emily. "It is she who has taken your parents."

"What do you mean, *taken*?" Emily shouted. Tarquin jumped bolt upright at the noise.

"Someone signing himself, 'your faithful servant, Peregrine' sent a note, addressed to my sister. He has an 'old nag and her feisty husband in chains.'" The Library's voice changed to a languid posh drawl Emily recognized as she channeled the writer's words. "But he, 'missed both child and the prize due to having Pooka troubles.' Your parents, I presume?"

"Yes! Why didn't you say this to begin with?" said Emily from between gritted teeth.

"Because the note has only just been written," the Library said, as if it was obvious.

"Why does she want my mom and dad? How do we get them back?" Emily was lion-fierce now and wanted to kick somebody right in the shins.

"The Nocturne wants what she always wanted. Freedom from the Midnight Hour. She took your parents to further that aim. She must hunt you for the same reason." The Library raised a hand, palm out, like a priest giving a blessing. "If you would rescue your parents, you must first stop the Nocturne."

"Er. What?" said Emily.

"You must find out her plans and stop them, like your mother before you. The Nocturne threatens the Hour, I know it."

Emily stopped dead. Shin-kicking plans were canceled.

"You have got to be kidding."

"It must be you."

"My name's not flippin' Frodo!"

The Library tilted her head in confusion, but Emily sailed on. "You must be loopy!" She cocked her thumb back at Tarquin. "Phone the Spooky Police or something. Send the Moon Army!"

"She cannot be defeated that way. As I am words, she is living music. All who hear her tune fall under her influence. An army would simply become hers. It must be you."

Tarquin was shaking his head, dumbfounded. This was one of the rare times Emily agreed with him.

"Why me? What's the matter with you people?" She was hopping mad now. How had this become her life? How?

"Because you can resist her. So few can, but your bloodline is special. You are . . . difficult, as is your mother."

"I'm not flippin' difficult!" she shouted.

The Library just looked at her.

"Oh, right. I suppose so." Emily kicked a shelf, hard. "I still can't do it! Why does everybody want me to do mad things on my own?"

As they argued, the Library had started to slump, her weight making the shelves creak as she leaned on them. She twitched her head this way and that, as if hearing voices again.

In the corners of her eyes, tiny black tears had started to trickle down her cheeks.

"Please, you must stop her. She cannot leave without magic. I fear she plans to . . ." She trailed off.

"Plans to what?" said Emily.

The Library did not answer, but stared around until she saw them, and started with surprise. "I–I . . . are you here?"

"Yes! This can't be the plan. You have to get someone else to help me. Please."

The Library's mouth flapped without sound and her eyes started to fill up with black again. From this close, it became clear what it was: words, endless tiny words, in all languages, swirling in ink through her eyes. The Library spoke once more, her voice little more than the rustle of pages.

"Start with the clock. It holds the answer."

"No! Just help me get my mom and dad back. At least tell me where they are?"

Emily knelt in front of her and grabbed her hand. As she did, the Library's eyes filled all the way to the top with black ink, and her face changed to that of something cunning and malicious.

"Far out of reach; prettier than ever; admired by all who see her. Do you feel that you have lost her?" She spoke in a cruel voice, unlike her own.

Emily let out a wail and let go. Tarquin put a gentle hand on her shoulder.

"She's gone again. Come away, this isn't a good place to be now."

As she and Tarquin inched back, the Library floated up and, seizing the nearest book, drifted down the corridor without looking back, lost in memories, speaking the words that consumed her.

CHAPTER 13

Emily crashed out of the huge museum doors and was halfway down the steps before Tarquin emerged behind her. She turned back to him and spread her arms wide.

"What just happened?" Her hands were shaking with anger. "I thought you said she was in charge? She's absolutely bonkers!"

The light of Tarquin's eyes flickered brighter.

"She is less than she was, true, but she founded this sanctuary with great sacrifice, and guards us all. Her words have merit."

"Her words are mental! What am I supposed to do now?" She stomped down the rest of the steps and flung herself onto a bench by the outer wall. She was about to start slamming her heel back against the wood when Tarquin hiked his cape up and sat down by her.

"You heard her. If you're to regain your parents, you must foil this plot."

She jammed a hand in her pocket. At least the Hog was a steady point of sanity and warmth, although she suspected he might have had a wee in there.

"How can you say that? I'm not going to fight the Knockers or whatever her name is."

"The Nocturne, who once was Music."

"Oh great. I repeat, *not* going on a quest." She poked him. "I just want to get my folks and go home."

He nodded.

"I understand. My people also take family seriously. It does you credit." He stood up again. "I understand being far from home, too."

Their eyes met. He nodded his head, making a decision.

"I think we should try and investigate at least. Perhaps you could locate them that way, then maybe the Watch can help after that."

"We?" Emily squinted at him.

"I'll help. You are my prisoner, after all." His mouth twitched into half a grin as he spoke.

"Was that an attempt at humor, Violet? This is not the

time." She maintained her grumpy expression, but it was a struggle.

"Unless you want to wait for the scent to wear off and get eaten by the Bear instead?" He held his hand out and, after a second's hesitation, she grabbed it, and he pulled her to her feet.

They walked out of the museum's courtyard and back onto the almost deserted street. It was quiet around here compared to most of the city. As she walked along, Emily had to step out of the way of a huge black dog with red eyes that trotted up the pavement, whistling. Wait, could dogs whistle? She turned back but it was gone around a corner. She caught up to Tarquin.

"Right then, it's all something to do with the clock. Let's just go to Big Ben and figure it out."

"We can't just *go* there. It's the most important place in the whole Hour, and completely restricted." He shook his head. "If someone of your background tried to get near it, I dread to think–"

"What do you mean, my background?" she said.

He flushed a deeper color again and the glow from his eyes dulled.

"Well, it's just that being from out there, Day Folk, as we would say . . ."

"What's that other thing I keep getting called? 'Daysie,' is it?"

He grimaced.

"That's not a very nice word, and only not-very-nice people would use it."

"I don't understand. Why are people so anti my world?"

"They're not, not all of them, but there's some ill-feeling out there, because we were forced to leave." He was examining the tips of his boots with great interest as he spoke. "I'm afraid some of my people think of your kind as, well, monsters."

"*What?* But that's . . . you're . . ." she spluttered.

He nodded in sympathy.

"I know, it's completely unfair. You were just misguided, clearly. You destroyed all the magic in the world out of blind ignorance and stupidity, not actual malice."

Even spluttering was beyond her this time.

"Either way, one of the Day Folk approaching the Great Working . . . it would not end well. There are combat sorcerers on guard. Zap! Frog. Most unpleasant."

Fair enough. The only thing that might make the day worse was if she had to eat flies for dinner.

"What are we going to do, then?"

"We'll have to investigate elsewhere. Like detectives."

He beamed at the thought, all of a sudden very young in his uniform. It would have been sweet, if he wasn't excited about them chasing some musical nightmare from the dawn of time.

"You know," said Tarquin, "it's odd that she said 'clock.' We never call it that. It's always 'the Great Working.' Hmmm . . . I wonder if that means something?"

"All right, Sherlock, who built the clock bit?"

"I don't know exactly. A coven of our wisest sorcerers and alchemists." Tarquin shook his head. "I *do* know they all went mad afterward, though. It was another brave sacrifice."

"Eh? How come?" said Emily.

"We need magic to survive, but everybody knows doing big magic is bad for you. It's why witches end up going a bit . . . gingerbread." He gestured in Big Ben's direction. Even from here the green glow lit the sky. "The Great Working was the biggest magic of all."

"Oh." Emily stopped walking and leaned against a mushroom-covered wall. Behind Tarquin, three large plants, giant Venus flytraps, dragged themselves along the pavement by their roots.

"This is useless. We can't talk to them if they've all gone bonkers."

"I wonder if we've got anything on file at the Night Watch . . ." He paused, face lost in thought, and his hand tapped a pocket in his uniform where a silver chain disappeared inside it. ". . . Watch, clock . . . Night Watch! I'm an idiot."

"I'm not arguing."

He didn't even notice.

"Yes, that's it. I know someone we can talk to. Cornelius Snark. He does work for the Night Watch, and I think he was involved with the Great Working."

Emily bounced up off the wall. The fungus behind her burst into a spreading cloud of multicolored spores, and the walking plants snapped them out of the air with long, purple whip-tongues.

"Where is he?"

"He's over in Whitechapel at the Bell Foundry. We'll need to walk down toward the main road to get a hackney carriage."

Emily favored Tarquin with a grin. He flushed with pride.

"Great. Let's go. It's a good thing he hasn't gone bonkers like the rest of them."

"Ah." Tarquin turned away. "I never said *that*."

They walked down from Bloomsbury, back toward Oxford Street. Emily started to have a prickling, static-electric sensation on the back of her neck. When she turned around, the big black dog from up by the museum was walking down the street behind her. It was definitely the same one, as it had a blaze of white in the middle of its black head. It was also definitely staring at her with its glowing red eyes.

"Erm, Tarquin?"

"Yes?"

As she spoke, the dog stopped, grinned a big, pink, doggy grin full of teeth, then turned and walked through the open door of a pub. She could have sworn it winked before it did, too.

She was about to tell him what had happened, when he jumped into the road and waved his hands up and down. Was he trying to take off? A giant black coach, pulled by spectral horses, all flame-eyed and see-through bones, screeched to a halt in front of him. A huge and ominous figure, with bolts through his neck and jagged stitches in his forehead, loomed up from the seat.

"Where to, guv'nor?"

Now they were rattling through the busy streets toward Whitechapel. She was saddened to discover that cushions hadn't been invented yet, and every cobble they bounced over imprinted itself right onto her butt. It was not improving her mood.

With time to think, the tidal wave of strangeness she was experiencing was starting to freak her out. A moonlit monster world was one thing, but her parents not being normal was quite another. (Well, her mom had never been normal, but this was a whole new level.) What did it mean that her mom was some kind of secret agent? Worse, that she had been there before the Midnight Hour. What did *that* mean? She did have some wrinkles, but there wasn't much gray under her multicolored hair dyes. How old could she be? Was she . . . Night Folk?

Even so, it was easier to imagine her mom as coming from a different world than it was to imagine her dad as . . . well, as more than her dad. How was her clinically boring dad in charge of "Dangerous Deliveries" for a magical midnight post office? Japonica had sounded proud, and that wasn't an emotion Emily associated with him at all.

Her hand worked at her neck, gripping the pennies through her T-shirt and grinding them together. None of it made sense, and as the moonlit surroundings slipped by outside the window, everything she knew to be true was slipping away, too. Who were her parents? If they had always lied, or at least never told her the whole truth, then who was *she*? It was too much right now. She wanted to be anywhere rather than here. If only everything would go back to normal.

During this mental avalanche, Tarquin had taken it upon himself to explain what Cornelius did for the Night Watch. The excitement of the mission from the Library and the general super-importance of everything that was going on had brought out the eager schoolboy in him. This was not helping her mood, either.

". . . So, it's always midnight here, you see, but it's not always midnight out there, in your world." He was waving his hands around. "When it's midnight in both places at the same time, that's when the doors that exist in both places open, for the length of the bongs."

He paused, awaiting a response. She made a grunting noise in the hope he'd stop talking. It didn't work.

"It is the calling of the Watch to guard our borders, so we must know when the doors are open."

He paused again. Another grunt.

"And thus . . ." Tarquin said with great ceremony, as he rooted around in the pocket of his uniform that the silver chain disappeared into.

". . . We *are* the Night Watch and this . . ." He pulled out the chain and something round and shiny dangled off the end. ". . . *is* a night watch!"

In his hand, he held a large silver fob watch case, attached to the end of the chain. It was engraved with a whirl of symbols and lines, like a shiny clamshell. Emily tipped her head on one side and glared at him.

"Right."

Tarquin flushed.

"It's a, well, it's a play on words, you see. I'm in the Night Watch, and this—"

"I get it. Great. Nice one." She scowled at her reflection in the window.

"I don't think you do. This is what Cornelius makes for us to show the time in both worlds. Look."

There was an indistinct clicking, as of tiny clockwork, and then a faint musical noise. Tarquin had opened the lid of the watch and held it flat in his hand. Now, a miniature version of Big Ben concertinaed impossibly out of the flat case, and stood eight inches tall. It was very *real* somehow, and rippled with a green witchlight. As he turned it, the various clock faces each showed a different time. The musical sound became clearer now. It was the one, two, three, four, quarter chime of the clock.

"All through this hour, Lord be my guide; that by thy power, no foot shall slide." She whispered the words as the chime sounded again, and her mom was with her, just for a moment.

"Ah, we have different words." He sang in a light, clear tenor. "All through this night, moon be my faith, and by its light, all shall be safe."

They smiled at each other, and the cloud of her bad mood passed on.

The coach rattled to a stop and the cabbie banged the roof with a massive hand.

"We're here," Tarquin said, and opened the door.

"Hey, do you think you *had* better perfume me again, in case it does wear off? I don't want to get eaten."

"I was joking," said Tarquin as he got out.

"Oh good."

"Yes, I'm not sure if it'll ever wear off, actually."

"WHAT?!"

CHAPTER 14

There was a distant, sonorous murmur of chimes and the occasional loud bong, well before they rounded the corner to the Bell Foundry. Behind double-height doors was a cavernous room filled with the throbbing heat of a furnace and BELLS! Bells were everywhere. Big bells, small bells, bronze bells, iron bells, bells split in half, bells hung from the roof on heavy chains, bells stacked on pallets, bells being polished with great care, or tapped with tiny hammers. Their gentle sound echoed all around as the movements of the place made them sing.

A bandaged mummy glanced up from shining a small golden bell as they came in. One look at Tarquin's uniform, and its duster-wrapped hand pointed to the back of the workshop. Emily followed Tarquin as he weaved through the hot iron and noise, then ran straight into him when he stopped dead.

He was gawping at another version of Big Ben, this one the size of a grandfather clock. It stood on an enormous workbench, and a crowd of tiny men dressed in brown boiler suits clambered all over it. They were each no more than six inches tall and had matching beards and sour expressions. Alongside, a hefty six feet of angry werewolf in a tweed vest and spectacles towered over them, supervising, and (literally) barking orders. The little men held shards of a shattered mirror. They were using them to angle moonlight from a window in the roof onto the grandfather clock, and also a small, empty, silver watch case that lay beside it. The case was the very image of the one Tarquin had just shown her.

Tarquin bit his lip.

"Probably better if I introduce us first."

"Oh, after you."

He edged into the werewolf's line of vision.

"Erm, Doctor Snark, I'm Constable-in-Training Postlewhite from the Watch. Can we talk to you, plea–"

The werewolf snarled, gave him a talk-to-the-paw gesture, and turned back to the clock, which the little men were now hammering at with tiny tools. Tarquin retreated. Some of the little men were definitely jeering at him.

"Good job," Emily said.

"I, he's . . . well, he's famously difficult."

"So am I."

She marched forward, sticking her chin out. Her tummy was doing flip-flops, though. He was *very* big and hairy. It didn't help that all the little men had stopped work and were nudging one another and watching. She flushed, but stepped up and tugged the edge of the werewolf's vest.

"Excuse me, Doctor Snarl or whatever, I've got to speak to you, it's very important."

He ignored her, so she tugged harder. His rabid gaze fastened on her.

"Do you," he growled, big teeth mangling his words, "have any idea how hard it is to get THIS into THAT?" He gestured at the big clock and then to the tiny watch case.

"Erm, what, no? That'll never fit in there."

"I KNOW, THAT'S WHY IT'S SO HARD!" he roared, covering her in a fine spray of dog spit. "INTERRUPTIONS MAKE IT HARDER. NOW GO AWAY!"

Emily was sure he was going to bite her, but he just turned back to his work. All the tiny men rolled around, clutching their stomachs with laughter and banging one another on the back. She wiped the spittle off her face, and a fire grew inside her. She snarled like an animal herself and swept a number of tiny cackling men out of the way with her arm. As a horrified

Tarquin leapt to stop her, she snatched the watch case out of the reflected moonlight. There was a discordant bonging from within the clock, and all of the mirror shards cracked at the same time. The outraged werewolf turned to her, all his fangs showing.

"WHAT HAVE YOU DONE?!"

"LISTEN, FUR-FACE," she shouted. "This is the least of your clock problems! The Library sent us because her sister is up to something with Big Ben—I mean, your flippin' Great Working!"

The werewolf towered over her, snarling, fangs bared and claws out. All the little men were backing off and hiding behind things. Oh dear, what a stupid way to die. She'd always wanted a dog, too . . .

The werewolf tipped his head to one side, and his ears pricked up.

"Repeat that," he said in a voice still half growl but less frenzied.

"I said the Nocturne is up to something that involves the Great Working."

"Well, why on earth didn't you say so?"

"Once again, I must apologize. It's been a difficult time."

Emily had perched on a corner of the workbench, while a

shamefaced Cornelius paced in front of her. Tarquin had his pad and pen poised, every inch the detective. Cornelius had sent the little men off on a "Brownie Break" but they still peered out from in between the piles of arcane scrap all around the workshop.

"I'm ashamed. I truly am. It's just with the full moon being permanent now, I'm in wolf-shape all the time. It's dreadful. I haven't had a cup of tea without hair in it for over a century. My temper's gone to pot."

He sighed, and his ears drooped. Emily had to restrain a strong urge to scratch his head.

"Well, I'll let you off if you can help us with the clock."

Cornelius's ears pricked up.

"Yes, yes. My specialist area, of course. I charmed the bells, did I mention?"

He *had* mentioned it several times already, but Emily smiled and nodded. *Who's a good boy, then? Yes, you are.*

"How is the Great Working involved, and why does the Nocturne want you? A conundrum." Cornelius stroked his chin fur in thought.

Tarquin smacked his hand on the bench, causing a chorus of "Ois" from the miniature workforce smoking pipes beneath it. "We know she wants to escape from the Midnight Hour. It must be to do with that!"

Emily made a face at him. "But she *can* get out! That

flippin' Bear already has. It chased me up the street with its stupid magic umbrella!"

Cornelius's ears flicked again.

"A Night Shade! Necessary for any magic outside."

Emily's brow wrinkled.

"So . . . why doesn't she just use the Night Shade, then?"

"Ah ha! Because she's a . . ." He clicked his claws, and bared a significant row of teeth, stuck for a word. "You know, great big things, endless amount of them in the sea—use them for lamp oil and women's support doodahs." He gestured at his sides.

"Whales?" said Emily with horror as she recalled an old history lesson.

"That's the ones!" said Cornelius, his tail wagging.

"She's a whale?"

"No, but would you keep one in a teacup?" said Cornelius.

"What?" said Emily. She was going to have a good sit-down somewhere quiet after this conversation was over.

"She's huge, huge!" Cornelius stretched his arms out, a fisherman showing the size of the biggest thing he'd ever caught. "Magically, at least. She's quite petite, in the flesh, as I remember. Yes, indeed."

He stared off into the distance, until Emily coughed.

"Ah yes. She needs an ocean of magic to keep her going and that's all inside here. Some umbrella made with a teacupful of midnight charm just isn't going to cut it."

Cornelius started to stride back and forth as he explained.

"Without the magic contained within the Midnight Hour, an Older Power such as the Nocturne would turn to dust on the wind in an instant. She cannot leave, for it would be her doom."

"Then what is she planning? The Library said she thought the clock was at the heart of it," said Tarquin.

"And what has it got to do with me and my mom and dad?" said Emily.

Cornelius flopped back into a grimy old armchair at the end of the workbench, causing a scattering of tiny, shouting men from beneath it.

"I have not a clue."

Emily groaned and put her head in her hands.

"Fret not, we will reason it through. I relish a challenge." He rubbed his furry paws together. "Why is she after you? What do you represent? Do you carry anything of moment from the Daylight realm?"

Emily left her face in her hands while she replied.

"Only my Hoggins, my mom's necklace, and some chip sandwiches."

"Hrrrrmmmm . . . Do you have the items mentioned?"

"Yes. Well, not the sammies. I ate them." Emily groped in her pocket. "Hog, meet Cornelius."

The Hog nestled in her palm and opened an eye. He looked Cornelius up and down, nodded once, and went straight back to sleep.

"Sorry, he's been busy."

"A most venerable beast and clearly sagacious, but I see no reason for his pursuit. The necklace?"

"Oh, yeah, here."

She tugged her T-shirt down and pulled the coins out. Cornelius leaned in, then reared back.

"By the great old ones!"

His ears had gone flat, and his hackles were raised.

"What? It's just Mom's old lucky necklace."

"Indeed! Lucky, you say? Could you just hold them out?"

Cornelius pushed his chair farther back as he spoke, but still leaned forward, fascinated. Emily unclipped the necklace and dangled the coins out in front of him.

"So, merely out of curiosity, has anything terrible happened to you recently? Piano landed on you, that sort of thing?" said Cornelius.

"I just told you my parents have been kidnapped!"

"Mrrrrrmm, peripheral but not personal enough. Anything else?"

"A demonic bear chased me! That was pretty personal."

"Ah! Did it catch you? Rip any bits off?"

He studied her for missing limbs, frowning.

"No! What's the matter with you? Do you *want* me to have had an accident?"

"You misunderstand. Answer me this: Have you experienced any direct, ghastly, personal misfortune since wearing that necklace?"

He got up and started to rummage in one of the drawers under the workbench.

"S'pose not. Apart from my whole life disintegrating," she muttered.

"Then something is very wrong." He produced a set of black metal feathers and, with notable caution, held them out toward the coins. "These were your mother's, you say?"

"Yeah, she wore them every day."

"Ah! Was her life riven with horrific and regular tragedy?"

"Only from her taste in clothes."

The feathers were making an angry-beetle-ticking noise.

"Her legs didn't fall off, though?"

"NO!"

As she shouted, the feathers went from black to gray, then turned to ash and dust and sifted down onto the floor. Cornelius held the stubs up and gazed at them with wonder.

"Well, I never."

He screwed his face up and threw his head back like he

was going to howl, but then just coughed and adjusted his spectacles.

"I specialize in the alchymic science of the charming of metals, so you can believe me when I tell you those coins are a potent charm of malignant fortune." He tapped his furry finger against the end of his snout, deep in worrisome thought. "They are a terrible force of bad luck, and I suspect to even touch them would bring instant and terrible misfortune. Wearing them is beyond most people's imagining."

Tarquin sat open-mouthed. He, too, inched away from her.

"The Bear said I smelled of bad luck . . ." she said. "Wait, so why can I touch them, then?"

"No idea." Cornelius beamed. "It's fascinating." He started to rummage deeper in the drawers behind, pulling out complex implements of brass and crystal. "Perhaps you're some kind of anti-magic vortex?"

"Is that a thing?" said Emily.

"No, I just theorized it right now," said Cornelius, as he squinted at her through a device that resembled a cross between a telescope and a robot spider.

"Made it up, you mean."

"Speculation is all part of the alchymic method, young man," said Cornelius, as he frowned down at the telescope-spider and banged it on the table.

"Lady," said Emily.

"What?"

"I'm a *girl*!" she said and jumped off the bench.

"In trousers?" Cornelius sniffed the air. "How extraordinary. Of course, you all look the same to me."

He discarded the telescope and waved a long silver fishing rod–looking thing at her.

"Could be anti-magic; could be a powerful force of good luck countering the bad luck. Are you especially lucky?"

"I just told you about my week!"

"Good point." He glanced at the fishing rod, sighed, then dropped it on the desk. "Hmmm . . . could be an equally vast force of bad luck acting as a counterweight, but it seems unlikely. I'm sure you'd know about it if you were a beast of ill-omen. Ha!" He shook his head. "No, I simply don't know, but the coins and your ability to carry them must be what they're after. I wonder why?"

As he spoke, Emily leaned back onto the workbench and the dangling coins in her hand brushed the grandfather clock Big Ben. It quivered, rocked, bonged with racing speed to thirteen, then all the faces sproinged off with great force, bobbing and clattering, like mad glass cuckoos on the end of long springs.

Emily, Tarquin, and Cornelius all looked at one another.

"Oh."

CHAPTER 15

Emily and Tarquin walked out of the Bell Foundry in silence. She wandered down the street, not caring where she went, and the slope of the hill took her down toward the Tower of London. Tarquin paused at a hatch in the wall, grabbed a grubby cone of newspaper filled with fish and chips, and handed it to her. She eyed the steaming food with suspicion then started to shovel it in with her fingers, without checking if it was made of three-headed fish or magic potatoes or anything. She didn't taste it as she chewed, but the food filled the hole inside her.

They sat on a wall alongside the Thames, which had a lot more sea serpents and merfolk in it than at home. She was pretty sure Tower Bridge was missing, too, but didn't have the heart to bring it up. She couldn't even finish her chips. She poked one into her pocket for the Hog, then sat unmoving as the moon-silvered water flowed past.

"Can you say something? I've not heard you stop talking before, so this is unnerving," said Tarquin.

"I just don't know anything."

"We do know something. It's to do with the coins. They want *them*, not you."

Emily pulled her knees up and wrapped her arms around them, and didn't answer.

"You heard what Cornelius said after he'd stopped howling about the clock," Tarquin said. "They're bad, but there's no way they can destroy the real Great Working. It's much too powerful for that. Anyway, it sounds like only you and your mom can pick them up."

A knot of hot lead flared up in her stomach when he said that. She didn't want to think about it.

"I don't care. Everything I know about everyone and everything is wrong." The words were thick in her mouth. "I can't cope with any more."

"I know it's difficult being somewhere strange. You mustn't give up."

"You have no idea how I feel!" she snarled. "And I don't need a motivational lecture right now, thank you, Tarquin!"

"My name is Tarkus actually." He stood up. "Tarkus Poswa. We changed it when we came here. To fit in."

He waited, hands laced so tightly together his knuckles went white.

"Oh. Right. Erm . . . well, it's a definite improvement on Tarquin, I'll give you that."

"Our country wasn't safe anymore, and this place was. We had no choice." As he spoke, he reached into his jacket, pulled out a bunch of dandelions, sighed, and bit the head off one. "I'm just saying I know how it feels when everything falls out from under you, that's all."

Her cheeks flushed with heat. "Okay, well, maybe you do know–LOOK OUT!"

She dived forward and grabbed at Tarkus as a big black post bike dropped out of the air where he'd been standing, and screeched to a halt right by them. The rider, a tall woman with owl eyes, a beak, and a white-feathered face, slid off in a smooth, weightless move. The owl-lady stretched, her neck turning much further around than it should have done. She looked at Emily, who had eyes as wide as an owl's herself.

"Express delivery for yoooo-hoo." She pulled out a small purple envelope from her leather shoulder bag, her fingers gnarled into black talons at the ends.

"Haven't had one of these for an age. They cost a fortune. Whoo are yooo then?"

"Erm, Emily?"

"I know *that*. The stamps wouldn't have brought us here otherwise, would they, nestling?"

Her beak opened in what Emily hoped was a smile, revealing thick pink gums and a pointy black tongue.

"I mean, whoo are yooo to be getting a letter in the grandest way, from the grandest house in the land? Last time I did one of these, it was to the Prince Regent himself."

She puffed her feathers out, then deflated again.

"Shot at me before I landed, tooo. Thought I was a grouse."

She still held the letter out of reach. Emily, who was fascinated by the "oooo-ing" but too scared to risk a joke, elected to go with the truth.

"I don't know who I am anymore."

The owl-lady cocked her head to one side. The huge eyes were bright and warm.

"Takes us all a while to figure that one out, fluff. Sometimes yooo fly a long way from the nest, only to find out you're still the shape of the egg yooo hatched from, eh?"

"Erm, if you say so."

"I doooo. Here." She handed Emily the letter, smiled again, and turned away. Emily didn't want her to go, though.

"My, my dad's a postie, too. A Night Postman."

The owl-lady turned her head all the way around to look back over her shoulder.

"Whooo?"

"His name's Alan Featherhaugh."

"Yoooo don't say?" The head spun back around with a quiet laugh. "If that's the shape of your egg, then you'll be fine, no matter how far you fly."

She flitted onto the bike, and flapped a weightless, feathered hand at Emily.

"Good hunting, little one."

And with that, she was gone into the air.

The envelope was a rich, thick purple silk. The front had "Emily Connolly" written on it in an ink silver as moonlight. It was her name, but mixed up with her mom's maiden name. She'd never been called that before. In the corner was a huge bloodred stamp with a fierce-faced woman on it, the same as the ones she'd seen in her dad's drawer.

"Ooh, a Bloody Mary, I've read about those. Very rare," said Tarkus.

"Eh?"

"The stamp. Very rare. They get magically delivered to anyone they're sent to, anywhere, as long as you have a true name." He peered with fascination at the stamp. "They even work outside the Hour. Aren't you going to open it, then?"

"I suppose so."

She didn't want to. While it still remained shut, nothing else was going to happen. But her mom and dad were still prisoners . . . She sighed and flipped the envelope over to get her thumbnail in under the hunk of black sealing wax on the flap at the back. She levered it open, wincing as the envelope's silk ripped. Inside was a thick, creamy-colored card, embossed with an emblem that was all scrollwork and pointy teeth. The motto beneath said, "Omnia Bibenda," which was all Greek to her but sounded posh and ominous. The blank space of the card was written over in green ink in elaborate, old-fashioned handwriting.

Sweet Child,

This has all been a Terrible and regrettable Misunderstanding. I have simply been Distraught and desperate to recover my Beloved heirloom Coin collection, stolen from me long ago, and my Servants have taken it upon themselves to act in my Name. Things have gotten Terribly out of Hand, and we regret the Unpleasantness that has occurred. I assure You your Family are in safe hands, but It affects our Tender heart to think of you Alone without them in Unsafe territory.

I am staying with loyal friends at the Address below. Let us meet there to discuss the Situation. The Ancient Law of Truce applies so you can come in perfect Safety. I'm sure We can soon Effect a return of the dearly Beloved items we are both currently Missing and get you back home to Safety as soon as Possible.

Yours,

From she called by men, the Nocturne.

There was an elaborate curlicued decoration printed across the bottom of the card, and beneath that just one word, in thick gothic lettering:

Tarkus, unashamedly reading over her shoulder, let out a low whistle.

"Blimey."

Emily blew out a long, sighing breath.

"What's Dunlivin when it's at home?"

"It IS a home. One of the grandest in the land. It's the family bier of the Stabville-Chests," said Tarkus.

"Beer?"

"*Bier*. You know, thing you lie down on in a tomb? It's the home of one of the Deadest families in England."

Emily groaned.

"I know I'm going to regret asking, but 'deadest'?"

Tarkus was nonplussed. "Well, you know, 'Deadest.' They've been Dead much longer than other people, so that makes them . . . better. They can trace their graves all the way back to the Impaler. They're frightfully grand."

He looked into the middle distance, face wistful. "It's the deceasing, there's just no substitute."

"Just stop. Where's this house, then?"

"It's a mausoleum, and it's in Chiswick. Gosh, I'd love to see it." He shook his head. "It's a pity we can't."

"What do you mean, can't?"

He smiled at her.

"Well, it's obviously a trap, isn't it? She will have to stick to the Law of Truce, that's ancient magic, but I bet she's got something dreadful planned, anyway."

"Yep. Don't care. Let's go and see her and give her these stupid coins."

"Oh ho!"

He gave her an admiring look, then leaned in, intent.

"Right, I get it. Say no more. What's the plan?"

Emily squinted at him.

"I don't have a plan. I'm giving her the pennies back and getting my mom and dad."

He smiled and tapped a finger to his nose.

"Ah ha, so we get fake coins, and then—"

"No!" Emily stamped her foot in frustration. "I'm giving her the real pennies, getting my mom and dad, and we're leaving."

"But, but, we have a mission!" He was doing his bulgy-eye face again.

"*You* might. I have something more important: a life, and I want it back."

She was worried his eyes might pop.

"But your mother defended the—"

"I don't care." Emily rubbed her face with both hands, then looked him straight in the over-bulging eyes. "I'm sorry, but none of this creepy old world is my problem. I want my mom and dad safe, and everything to go back to normal. I'm not a hero. I just want to go home."

He stared at her, his face screwed up with disbelief.

"But she clearly wants them for something terrible. This could be part of a plan to destroy my whole world!"

"You heard Cornelius: The coins can't break the Great Working, and she can't leave. It'll be okay." As she said it, a flare of shame reddened her cheeks, but it wasn't enough to stop her.

"You're just saying that because you want it to be true! What if it's not?" His voice got louder and louder. "You can run off home, but my family lives here. All our families live here!"

"It's *my* family I care about right now! Are your mom and dad prisoners? Are they?" She was shouting now, too.

They stopped and faced each other.

"Look, I'll make sure it's all okay when I do the swap. I'll . . . I'll make sure."

He shook his head. Grave determination came to his face. She had seen it before when he had put himself between her and the Bear's gang.

"I can't let you do this."

"What are you going to do, perfume me?" She took a step back regardless.

"No, I'm taking them to safety."

As he spoke he lunged at her and grabbed the necklace. His nails grazed her skin and pain burned in her neck as he yanked her forward.

"Argh!"

He was so close that the coarse, dark-blue fabric of his uniform pressed against her face. As he pulled sideways the necklace started to strangle her and, as she panicked, the hot liquidness started to form in her chest again, but then it was over. The pulling stopped, and she fell backward. She scrabbled around to fight him off, but he wasn't there. The necklace! For one dreadful moment she thought it was gone but a pat at her chest jangled the comforting touch of warm coins. Tarkus, though, had vanished.

"I think I've broken something."

His voice came to her all echoey and hollow.

"Have you gone invisible? Is that one of your things? You can't have them, you git." She spun around, hands out, feeling for anything coming at her.

"No, I'm down here."

Right in front of her, where they'd been struggling, invisible against the blackness of the night, was a large open manhole. Tarkus's voice was coming up from below.

"Oh god, are you . . . ?"

She leaned over and made out the faint glow of his eyes in the dark. He was a long way down and wedged against a wall at a funny angle. His constant background flowery smell was still present but there were a number of other odors wafting up, too, none of them good.

"How did you—"

"I touched the pennies, and the next thing I knew: wham! I think I might have slipped on a banana when I landed, too."

"Are you okay?"

His head bobbed as he tested his various bits.

"My ankle hurts but everything I landed on is soft. I don't want to know why."

"Okay, I'll get a rope—Wait, what am I saying?" She glared down the hole. "You just nearly strangled me, you twit. What did you think you were doing?"

"You can't take those coins to her. Look what just touching them did to me." He levered himself up and reached toward her. He was a long way from the manhole. "She must have something terrible planned. Please!"

She sat back from the hole and ran her fingers through her tangled hair.

"I promise, promise, that I'll make sure it's okay before I do it, but I have to get my mom and dad back. It's all my fault they're here."

She flung her hands out in annoyance.

"And I don't want to leave you in the hole, but you're

totally going to do something stupid if I try and get you out, aren't you?"

He folded his arms, jutted his jaw, and tried to look dignified, despite something brown dripping from his ear.

"My duty is clear."

"I knew it. You absolute idiot."

She sighed.

"Right, I'm sorry, Tarkus, I truly am, but you'll just have to stay there for a bit. I promise I'll tell someone to send help, but, you know, probably not immediately."

"You are making a terrible decision."

"We'll see, won't we? Don't suppose you want to tell me the way to Dunlivin, do you?"

His howl of outrage was answer enough.

"Thought so. Right, well, chin up, eh? Think nice-smelling thoughts."

From behind her, in the hole, came the most unusual noise—a wet, soggy, extended raspberry. Then, as the foul liquid cleared, the raspberry began to fade away, and soon a whistle began to peal out: Tarkus's whistle, clear and silver as the moonlight, calling the Night Watch to render help to an officer in need.

Pausing only to pick up her half-full cone of chips from the floor, Emily ran into the night.

CHAPTER 16

Well, *that* went well. How to win friends and influence people, the Featherhaugh way.

Emily picked her way through grimy streets and alleys along the Thames with yet another friendship set on fire behind her. All alone with no idea where she was going. She munched her last cold, miserable chip, licked her fingers, and looked around for somewhere to put the paper. There was a pile of trash in the mouth of an alleyway and no bins in sight, so she crumpled the cone up into a ball and tossed it on the pile.

She had turned away when the pile shifted and about half of it stood up, stretched, and yawned. It was a small . . . woman?

With an outfit made of trash and an odor to match. And now with a chip-paper hat.

She looked at Emily, her eyes narrowed in suspicion.

"You leaving that, then?"

"Oh, I'm *so* sorry, I just thought you, it, was a pile of tra—" She stopped before it got any worse.

"You don't want 'em, then?"

The little rubbish lady picked the paper off her head and sniffed it with relish.

"It's, it's just the paper."

"Just the paper, she says. There's good eating on there." She held the crumpled cone up between them. "Y'mind?"

"Erm, no, no, all yours."

The cone vanished inside the little woman's mouth before Emily had finished speaking. A dreadful chewing, slurping, and munching followed. It was impossible to look away. The little woman swallowed, burped, and rubbed her tummy.

"Aaaaah! Grand. That's the problem with the young today. Wasteful. You'll be throwing away bodies next." She grinned, showing a mouthful of sharp black teeth. "Good eatin' on them, too."

"I have to be going. Right now," said Emily.

She took two paces back toward the mouth of the alley, then stopped. "Excuse me, but do you know how to get to Dunlivin?"

"Ha! Easy, you just need to be rilly rich and rilly dead." The black teeth reappeared as she cackled.

"Great, thanks." Emily turned to walk away.

"Nah, luv. Just joking. S'on the river, in Chiswick, ain't it? You wants to get a wherry-boat down from Wapping wharf."

"Brilliant! Thank you!" Emily was already jogging down the road.

"Wait, hang on, you're not going there are ya? They're a right bad lot."

The little woman shook her head as Emily disappeared around the corner.

"Waste of a perfectly good body, that."

The wharf was mayhem. Denizens of all types milled around it, and the river beyond was busier than Emily had ever seen it back in her London. The water was hidden under an armada of different size boats, ships, and the occasional giant squid. Oars splashed, smoke poured from chimneys, and the water foamed as everything ploughed through with no regard for anyone else. It was pure watery chaos and she needed a way to travel down it.

There were a number of boats drawn up along the wharf, with signs and owners touting for trade. She rejected the ones that were too piratical or too hungry-looking and settled on a taxi-boat at the end of the row. It was three times the size of a rowing boat, with a small cabin at one end and a honking big steam engine and paddle wheel at the other. The captain was mainly a beard that filled the gap between a heavy oilskin coat and a battered stovepipe hat. He didn't appear to speak. He nodded when she asked for Chiswick, and then his whole beard twitched when she asked to be dropped near Dunlivin. She was sure he was going to refuse, but he motioned her aboard and pointed to the cabin. She pulled out the smallest of the notes she still had in her pocket, and he pressed a handful of warm, grubby coins back as change.

The ride was hair raising. The captain and his marine colleagues didn't care about anybody else on the river. The steam-powered boats roared past, and sometimes into, the unpowered boats; the little steam boats were at risk from the bigger paddle steamers that were the size of angry whales; and even the biggest steamers avoided the giant squid. In between all these were fins, tentacles, and the occasional leering merman, all black eyes and needle teeth. It was enough to put you off swimming ever again. She sat, teeth gritted, as the beard, which now had a large pipe jammed in it, tore down the river. The boat's chimney poured out smoke and smuts of ash into the night air, and she was glad the wind was going the other way.

As she sat and stared out at the banks rolling past, she saw movement out of the corner of her eye. Walking across the deck was a little girl in a nightie, clutching a furry penguin toy. Emily would have sworn she was the only passenger, though. Had the girl come from the engine room? She seemed unbothered by the splashing, the breeze, or the surrounding monsters, and pirouetted across the deck with her penguin in her own world. But it wasn't her own world; as she got closer, Emily could see straight through her. The girl was a . . . what had the angry potato man said? She was a *dreamling*. The pirouetting took her too close to the side, and Emily leapt up to grab her, but as she did, the girl was gone. Not into the water but just . . . gone. Emily sagged back into her seat, and turned to look at the captain. The beard slowly shook from side to side, then turned back to the wheel.

What were the dreamlings? Why were they here? Had she had dreams like that when she was little? She couldn't remember any. She decided to worry about it on a day when she wasn't heading into the jaws of certain doom instead.

An hour later they nosed in toward the bank and pulled up at a huge stone jetty. They only rammed two smaller boats, and knocked a fisherman screaming headfirst into the water, in the process. She breathed a sigh of relief and began to gather herself. The captain leaned back from the wheel, and the beard spoke for the first time.

"You sure this is where you wants to be, missy? They'se a

rum lot, the Stabville-Chests, I hear, even for the Hungry Dead." He paused and spat into the water. "Dun't seem right you going in all on your lonesome. Pardon me saying."

Emily smiled at the unexpected concern.

"Thank you. I . . . well, I have to, that's all." The beard bristled with worry and she wanted to reassure him. "I've got a hedgehog, though."

The beard bristled less.

"Well, that's summat at least. You go careful now."

The last she saw of him was a raised hand from his perch at the tiller, and a puff of black smoke as the engine clattered back into life and hissed and huffed the boat back into the current and straight over a small canoe. The little act of kindness from a man who didn't speak much made her tummy twist as it brought her dad vividly to mind. Her dad, who was quiet, too; her dad, who had always been there for her; her dad, who might not be boring after all. She wanted to sit in happy silence with him; she'd even have let him fuzzle her hair if he was there. But he wasn't, he was prisoner of some awful witch-thing, so she screwed her courage up and turned to face Dunlivin.

At the back of the jetty was a huge stone arch, supported on thick, fluted pillars, all carved from black granite. There was a great stone crest at the top of the arch, the same as on the letter, all pointy teeth and twirly bits. She steeled herself and walked through it, up some steps, and came out into a garden. There was a spread of manicured lawns and trees intersected with paths and statues and dotted with squared-off stones sticking up everywhere. It was a huge graveyard, she realized, with tombs scattered throughout, some as big as houses, with marbled angels on every corner. Wild horses wouldn't have dragged her into this type of place after dark at home, but it was peaceful after the rest of her endless, dreadful night.

The grounds started to change as she got closer to the top of a small hill. The graves stopped, and the green open space grew more decorative. The stone chips on the path changed to pure, glinting black, as did the color of all the flowers in the borders. The statuary on the corners and in the shrubberies grew bigger and more imposing—great fanged warriors battling angels or looming over innocents, all portrayed in black basalt stone. The whole place became monochrome, with the ever-present moonlight leaching any color from the grass and making the black elements of the garden glow.

She came to a huge expanse of grass with more black statues scattered across it. Hang on, they looked like . . . one of them put its head up and glared at her, making Emily jump straight up in the air with a squeak.

It was a flipping rhino. A herd of black rhino. Casually

on the lawn. Black rhino, black flowers, black, well . . . everything.

"You know what, Hoggins? I'm detecting a theme."

In the shock of the rhino, she'd missed the building behind them. It loomed, a mix between tomb and mansion. It had high arched church windows, a statue-lined path leading up to it, and a giant front door. There was no doubt this was her destination. Great. Not even slightly ominous.

The statues glared down at her as she approached, all knife-edge cheekbones and sharp fangs. In fact, they all resembled the Dracula lookalike the very naughty horse had flattened earlier. Had that been today? It was impossible to tell in this timeless place. It seemed a lifetime ago already. Names and dates were etched underneath the statues, but most were too faded to be legible. Which was presumably to let you know just how much more Dead they were than you.

The loud scrunch of gravel under her feet was unbearable by the time she'd reached the door. She was just about to yank the dangling iron bell-pull when the door screeched open. She shrieked and stumbled. A tall, thin man with a gaunt, sallow face, in a black jacket with tails, leaned out of the shadows within. He resembled a sour-faced daddy long-legs in a suit. He was about to speak when he was cut off by an outraged shout.

"You totally did that on purpose!" Emily yelled.

"Ma'am?" His voice creaked the same as the door had.

"You waited until I was about to ring the bell, then you jumped out at me! I bet you always do it." Emily loved an argument. As she ranted, the sense of dread that had been crawling up her back scuttled off to bother someone else.

"I assure you, ma'am—"

"Where's your little spyhole, then? Do you peer through and wait, or do you listen out for the gravel to crunch? I bet it's the gravel."

He might have been spooky, dead, and two hundred years old, but he'd never been shouted at by the gob before. She stepped forward, forcing him back over the threshold, wagging her finger in his face, and was in the hall before he regained his composure.

"I assure you, ma'am, it is simply a coincidence."

"My butt it is. I bet you keep score."

"Ahem. If ma'am would care to state her business?"

"Ma'am *would* care. I'm here to see . . ." Who was she here to see? The Nocturne, right, but was that her real name? What if it was actually, like, Nicky or something?

"Yesssss?" He steepled his fingers and arched an eyebrow.

"You know very well who I'm here to see. Jog on and get her."

She couldn't believe it had come out of her mouth. The butler widened his eyes, then inclined his head.

"Walk this way."

He turned and strode off without looking back to see if she was following. Emily bustled along behind his bandy, erratic stride, unable to hide a grin. She'd stood up to the butler by pretending to be braver than she was. Perhaps that was how bravery worked? If she just kept that up . . .

She nearly walked into his bony back as he stopped and opened a great black door in the wood-paneled hall they were in.

"If you'd wait in here please, ma'am? I shall fetch the Great Lady, and his lordship."

He ushered her in and was gone in a whirl of coattails and scrawny legs. The room was large and stark, dominated by an acre of empty wooden floor, one wall of tall windows looking out onto the rhino-filled grass outside, and a number of huge candle-filled chandeliers. Was it a ballroom? At the far end of the room were a chaise longue and a few other velvet chairs, drawn up next to a fireplace. Next to them was a wind-up gramophone with a giant horn, and a slew of old vinyl records around it, most out of their covers. She wandered over, drawn by their lurid colors. Who were the Bay City Rollers, or Ziggy Stardust? These people all had serious haircut issues. Who the heck was Thin Lizzy or The Clash? That one rang a bell; had her mom listened to them? They definitely weren't from 1859, anyway. Odd. Where had they come from?

There was a constant, low swirl of music, coming from nowhere Emily could put her finger on. Was she hearing things? She pressed her hands over her ears but it was still there. She sat down, got up again, chucked her bag on the chaise longue, hovered for a minute, then walked to the window instead. Rhino really were honkingly big. Emily tangled her fingers in the necklace of bad pennies under her shirt and jingled them as she waited. She put her other hand in her jacket pocket and the warm weight of the Hog shuffled into it. She pulled him out and brought him up to eye level.

"Hog, I've got to say, I'm pretty much wetting my pants here. I hope I'm doing the right thing."

He was, ever so slowly but very definitely, shaking his head from one side to the other.

"What's that supposed to mean?" she hissed. She'd have questioned him further but voices and footsteps were coming toward the door now. The haunting background music grew louder.

"Thanks a lot, Hoggins," she muttered, tucking him away in her pocket and turning to face the door.

It opened and the enormous bulk of the Bear filled the whole doorway.

"Girl," he growled, through a mouth sprouting more teeth as he talked. "No horse this time. MINE!"

CHAPTER 17

He loomed in the doorway and raised his huge, claw-tipped paws. Emily was certain she was going to be ripped to shreds, then a new voice cut through the Bear's ripsaw growling.

"Now, now, Ursus. That's enough." The Voice sounded beautiful, perfect even. Although the words had been spoken, not sung, it was melodic, sweet and fluting, and fell like music on the ear. Despite her terror, Emily wanted it to speak again.

"She is here by my invitation, so under the Ancient Law that binds us all, she is offered safe conduct."

It sounded even more beautiful this time. Emily was seized by a warm rush of affection for the owner of the Voice that was saving her. The owner was undoubtedly gracious and beautiful and good. Emily straightened up, unafraid. As she did the Bear lowered his killing paws and stepped back, his shaggy head bowed.

"Beg pardon," he mumbled.

"I should think so, too. We will resolve all this without such old-fashioned brutality. Let us talk as civilized people."

"Quite so, old chap." Another speaker now, with tones far less beautiful. They sounded braying and harsh in comparison. When would the Voice speak again?

The Bear shuffled away, contrite. As he did, the other people behind him came into view. First was the flattened vampire, still draped in his Transylvanian, opera-cape finest. He was a lot less flat now, but there were bumps and scratches visible on his pale skin. His flowing blond hair had been primped and arranged to cover a hoof-print on his temple. It wasn't him Emily was interested in, though, it was the owner of the Voice.

When she appeared, she was just as Emily had imagined. A perfect beauty, but kind, not austere. She was tall, with long, sweeping black hair, with a distinct thick streak of gray through it on either side, pinned back from her high forehead with silver combs. Her skin was pale and delicate, and her eyes a midnight blue. A graceful neck plunged into a dress the color of her eyes, which flared out into a billowing trail of pearls. She looked like the sea, and sounded like the wind, and Emily was entranced.

She took graceful steps toward Emily, who stood rapt in the corner. The lady spoke only one word, "Come," but it was enough to fill her up with its honeyed warmth. They sat by the fire, opposite each other, and the lady smiled and Emily smiled back, happy to be where she was.

"Now," said the Voice, and it was still beautiful, but not overwhelming with its glory, and Emily leaned forward to listen.

"Introductions. You, I know, are Emily, and I am very pleased to meet you at last."

Emily glowed with pleasure at that.

"I have lots of names," said the lady, and wrinkled her nose as if to show they were a burden. *How awful for her. Poor thing, with all those names.*

"For instance, I'm sure Lord Stabville-Chest here would think you should call me 'Great Lady,' as he does. Is that not right, Peregrine?"

The vampire was leaning, in an effortless, graceful pose, next to the fireplace.

"Well, it does seem appropriate given the difference in rank, Great Lady."

"Nonsense." The lady wrinkled her nose again and rolled her eyes at Emily. *See what I have to put up with?* Emily smiled back, happy to be conspired with. "No, that's far too stuffy." She leaned closer to Emily.

"My closest friends call me Melpo and I hope you shall, too."

She reached across and patted Emily on the knee, and Emily blushed. Melpo regarded her, lips pursed in concern.

"Oh, but, my dear, look at you." She turned back over her shoulder. "Burke, bring us tea, please. Young Miss Emily has not been looked after properly."

The butler, who Emily hadn't spotted lurking in the shadows, strode straight for the door, but was halted by that golden voice again.

"Oh, and some of those tiny cakes. The poor child looks starved."

Emily was in love. The tea came straight away, along with some excellent cakes, and the next few minutes passed in a dream. Melpo asked her about how she had traveled here and nodded with grave concern and real interest as Emily told of her adventures. Emily told her about some of the things she'd found out, about being chased by the Bear (who she curiously didn't care was sitting in the same room with them), and was just about to launch into talking about what her dad had done at the Night Post, when all of a sudden that odd, liquid sensation returned. But this time it was in her head, not her chest, a growing heat behind her ears.

The first time she'd been given tea and biscuits in this world it had been at the Night Post, by a demonic, red-eyed woman with talons, but that woman had been kind, had been a friend, and Emily had felt that to be true despite the evidence of her eyes. Now there was this woman, this beautiful woman with the perfect voice, who'd asked her to use a name reserved only for friends. Well, there was something just not right, and Emily could once again feel that to be true, no matter what the rest of her senses told her. Her head pulsed with the sensation, her story trailed off, and she put her hand in her pocket to cup the Hog and was then completely sure.

"No."

Melpo looked up from the teapot she'd just picked up, with an inquiring smile.

"No more tea?"

"No. No more of this. I don't know what you're doing, but it's not working anymore."

Out of sight in her pocket, she jabbed her finger down on one of the Hog's spikes until her eyes watered with the pain.

"I'm difficult. You can't affect me like other people. I know you're not my friend." As she spoke, the pain helped clear her head. "I've got something you want and you can't take it, and we both know it. So let's stop being nice."

Emily put her cup down and sat back, scared but exhilarated. She may have ruined the effect a second later by leaning forward to grab another cake in case they were taken away, but figured she was ahead on points whatever.

The Nocturne, for that's who she truly was, not nice Melpo, not the beautiful Voice, granted her a nod of respect.

"Your mother's daughter, I see." The voice was still musical and enticing but now it only swirled around Emily, not through her and into her heart. The distant music that had haunted the room hovered around the Nocturne like a cloud. She *was* music.

The Nocturne finished pouring herself some tea, and sat back with it, casting an assessing gaze over Emily as she did.

"Very well, child, let us talk without the veils. We each have something the other wants. How shall we trade?"

"Don't know why we do not just take," rumbled the Bear from his seat of shame in the corner. The Nocturne raised a finger without looking at him.

"Ursus, I shall not tell you again. There is Ancient Law that has bound us all since before we left the forest shadows, and it binds me as any other. An invite to the table opens the right of hospitality, and until the talk is done and boons and price agreed, all will be safe from harm."

The Bear subsided and the vampire, Lord Peregrine, smirked at his discomfort.

"So, name your boon, and your price." The Nocturne's eyes were now almost totally blue, barely a hint of white in them. She was less human than when she'd come in; it had dropped away from her when the Melpo guise did. Paler, thinner, and more vivid, she was the realest thing in the room, even against the heft of the Bear. Emily was a shadow in comparison. How had she ever imagined she could deal with this . . . Power? What was she doing?

"Boon?" she asked.

"The item or favor you want. What do you wish of me in exchange for my desire?"

"You've got my mom and dad, right? And they're okay?" She cringed at how pathetic she sounded.

A tiny movement of the head from the Nocturne. Yes.

"Why did you take them?"

"Is that your boon? Just that knowledge?" The Nocturne smiled without humor. Emily flinched. She was doing it all wrong!

"No! It's not. Wait, is this one of those three-wish things?" She waved the pointy finger of suspicion at the Nocturne.

A wrinkle formed in the perfect forehead, which was probably as close as the Nocturne got to looking frustrated.

"No, child. I am not a genie. You can ask for what you want, and I will ask for what I want, and we will make a deal, or we will not. It has been this way for more years than even I can remember."

I can remember . . . The Library had said she was losing herself in memories but the Nocturne was not somehow. She was certainly more together than the Library as she sat there, back straight and eyes bright. What had Cornelius called her? Magically huge. Those eyes stared at Emily, questioning and vast, and she had to look away.

"Well?" said the Nocturne.

It was the rigid tension of being put on the spot in class with a tough question. What was she meant to say? She wanted her mom and dad back, but this was all starting to sound tricksy. What if she said the wrong thing?

"Wait! What do *you* want?" Emily gabbled out, trying to buy some time to think. "You said we'll both say what we want. What's yours?"

The Nocturne inclined her head, a swan dipping its neck.

"A fair question. I want the coins, known in this age as the bad pennies, delivered unto me today, given freely and with no onus nor géis."

As she spoke, the pennies weighed heavy around Emily's neck, burning hot and cold and unseen under her T-shirt.

The Nocturne continued: "I would see them proved first, and I would have them given safely into my keeping in a manner that will not harm me." She smiled, but there was no warmth in it. "That is all I desire, from you at least."

"Why do you want them?" said Emily. She really didn't like the sound of that "at least." "Are you going to destroy Big Ben, the Great Working, I mean?"

"That, child, is knowledge beyond the terms of this

exchange. You may offer for it, but I do not have to tell you now." Emily started to speak, but the Nocturne raised a hand to stop her.

"I will say, as I see your heart is entangled in all this, that I seek only my own freedom, not the destruction of the great spell that holds my people. I will do no harm to it."

The Nocturne leaned in close.

"So, I ask, one final time. What boon do you seek in exchange for my desire? You will tell me now or, as is permitted by Ancient Law, our truce will end."

Everyone in the room stared at her, and she squirmed in her chair. The language the Nocturne had used was so complicated. What the heck was a "gesh"? How was she supposed to phrase what she wanted? She wasn't a lawyer.

"No, no, just hang on, I need to think."

The Nocturne was paler than before and her eyes were glowing sapphires. She was less human than ever. She was no longer the elegant woman who had taken tea, but a terrible and ancient thing. A wild and violent music crept into hearing, emanating from all around her, quiet but growing louder. She tapped one finger to it as she spoke, and her voice had changed to screeching violin strings. How had she ever appeared beautiful?

"The time to think is over. Speak your desire!"

CHAPTER 18

E rm, okay. Here's what I want . . ."

Oh god. Emily closed her eyes and tried to get it all in order, but the music skirled and whirled around her, and her nerves were on fire. It wouldn't all line up straight in her head.

"I–I want my mom and dad back, unharmed, and to be able to go home back to my world, the Daylight realm." She counted off points on her fingers as she spoke. "And for you not to do anything horrible to us while we're trying to go, or after. With no bonus or gesh, or whatever it was you said."

"Very well." The Nocturne started to nod.

"Wait, I'm not done," Emily gabbled over her. "I want

Tarkus and his family to be left alone, and the Hog, and for you not to do anything bad—"

The Nocturne held up a hand.

"This is not a Christmas list."

She narrowed her blue, blue eyes.

"I am prepared to grant the boons asked for so far regarding your family, and these others, and no more. Do not dream to dictate my actions."

Her eyes, which were full blue now, no whites, blazed bright at Emily, who shrank back in her chair.

"Okay."

"This is acceptable?"

"I—I suppose so, yes."

There was a horrible yawning worry she had forgotten something or messed it all up. The Hog was squeaking and ferreting around in her pocket. What had the Nocturne said exactly? The words were like a contract, so were there any loopholes or—

"Then we have made an agreement, and Ancient Law is satisfied, and we are each tied to surrender the boon offered."

She held a shimmering hand out. Emily hesitated, then held hers out, too. When the Nocturne touched her, it was so cold it burned. She flinched back with a yelp. Her hand must be black and . . . but there was nothing there, apart from a deep ache. The music had softened right down, and the room now echoed only to the Nocturne's cold voice.

"So then. Grant me my boon, child, and I will grant yours."

"Wait, how do I know you will?"

There was a trace of a smile, a real one, and in that moment she resembled the Library and it was possible to see them as sisters.

"Because these powers that bind us are older even than I, and I can no more cheat them than not be myself. Grant me my boon, child. Show them to me."

Emily inched her jacket open and pulled the necklace out from against her skin and laid it on top of her T-shirt. The distant background music flared up and became a howl before dropping away again. The Nocturne's eyes changed from the blue of glacial ice to that of a stormy sea, and her face showed the naked hunger of something starving.

"Yes."

Just one word but it contained lifetimes of longing. The Nocturne had eyes for nothing else, and the Bear and Peregrine were both leaning in to try and see.

"Go stand under the light, girl."

Emily stood up and walked a few paces toward the chandelier. The Nocturne's eyes never left the coins.

"Now prove them."

"What do you mean?"

"I would see them at work. I will not be bought for some trickster's fairy gold."

Emily rubbed her hand back and forth across them, all the staring giving her the fidgets.

"Erm. Someone needs to touch them, I think. To show the bad luck." Her head filled with Tarkus pleading with her from the manhole and his face as she'd left to do this idiotic thing. "It's pretty bad, though, you should—"

"Peregrine. Bring them to me."

The Nocturne's voice was cold as deep, dark water.

"Er . . . what? Sorry, must have misheard—" said the vampire.

"Bring them to me."

He twined his fingers in his cape.

"But, Great Lady, surely . . ."

The Nocturne gave him the benefit of her piercing gaze.

"They must be proved. Redeem with bravery your failure to bring them to me, Lord Stabville-Chest."

Peregrine was fidgeting on the spot now, the Bear's grin growing wider and wider behind him.

"Ah . . . they are indisputably meant to be quite nasty."

"Who better than our boldest then?"

At that he stiffened, and his chest puffed up within his cape.

"You're right, of course."

The Bear snickered.

In a flash of movement that Emily missed by blinking, the vampire was in front of her. It made her jump, and the coins jingle. Up close, he wasn't as handsome as the picture he presented from afar. His skin was parchment thin and yellowing, with white bone showing through it. His eyes were sallow and red-pupiled, and he stank of old blood and grave-mold. He leaned in close, his voice no more than a whisper.

"I haven't forgotten about your horse-tricks, you filthy nag."

Fangs crept from his mouth, as yellowed as his skin.

"Peregrine." The voice again.

"Right this instant, Great Lady. Come, child, render unto Caesar. Ha." The smile came again but behind it was a bad and rotting thing only playing at being human.

He held his pallid hand out and twitched the fingers. Gimme.

Emily reached back behind her head with both hands for the clasp, and all the times her mom had done the same thing came flooding back. All the times she'd taken the necklace off for Emily to play with, and all the times her mom had hugged her, and the necklace had been there at eye-height as she'd been held, and how the coins and their curious symbols and her mom's perfume all combined in her head to mean love, and she knew she was doing the wrong thing and there was no way to stop it happening. As the clasp came loose under her fingers, her memories came loose inside, too, and faded to black.

"Here."

Emily took a certain amount of pleasure in the way Peregrine dodged back as the pennies swung toward him. He braced himself and reached for them as though he was putting his hand into a fire. He took them with eyes and teeth gritted tight, and there was a moment in which she felt sorry for him. It didn't last long. He held them and nothing happened. Nothing happened for a bit longer and he turned back around to face the Nocturne, delicate as if he were holding dynamite.

"Right. I'll walk back over then. I imagine I'll trip and stub my toe or something, so you mustn't be alarmed, Great Lady."

In the corner of the room, the Bear had leaned forward and put his chin on both hands. All he needed was popcorn.

Peregrine set off, walking with exaggerated care, placing each foot deliberately on the smooth floor. Just before he passed under the chandelier, he looked up and bared his teeth in a grin, eyes agleam with cunning. The chandelier trembled, crystals swaying as it moved. He edged around instead of walking underneath it.

"Ah, you'll have to be cleverer than that!" He grinned his foul grin at the Nocturne, who sat watching him, her face impassive. "You know, I think a cunning man could best these accursed coins with care, Great Lady. Luckily, I am that cunning mAAAAAAARGH!"

He didn't finish his sentence because, in an explosion of wood and glass, one of the black rhinos charged straight through the wall of windows overlooking the lawn, straight across the ballroom, and straight through Lord Peregrine Stabville-Chest. It went on through the big door and into the hall, taking the mangled vampire with it on the end of its horn. The necklace fell to the floor where he'd been standing and glinted with malevolence. From within the house came the distant sounds of crashing and screaming.

Emily and the Bear sat, jaws agape. The Nocturne nodded once.

"Much as expected. They are proved, and you have near delivered your half of the bargain."

"Guh—rhino," said Emily, and added that to her list of useful things she'd said in moments of high drama.

The Nocturne produced a small silver box worked with intricate runic carvings. A press of a concealed catch and it popped open to show a velvet interior just the right size for the pennies.

"This box is charmed. It will allow you to complete your

part of the bargain and deliver them to me without harm. A good job I thought of it, or you'd have had to come along with us until you could." She wagged a warning finger. "The detail of these boons is very important. Now please put them into this."

"Why?"

The Nocturne scowled at her.

"Because we have a bargain."

Emily shook her head.

"No, I don't mean that. Why can't other people touch them? Why can I?"

A broad grin split the Nocturne's face. A sharp slice of white exposed bone in a wound.

"You have no idea what you are, do you, child?" She turned to the Bear, laughing. "She has no idea!"

They both laughed, the Bear's chainsaw gurgle and the musical trill of the Nocturne dancing around her.

"Stop it! Tell me!"

The Nocturne dabbed at her eye with a tiny handkerchief, still smiling.

"Do you have something else you wish to bargain with? Some other magic trinket, hmmm? Perhaps you'd trade your mother back again to know?"

Her smile faded and there was only malice on her face now. Emily looked away.

"No."

"I thought not. Onward then."

The Bear brought the little silver box over to Emily, giving the necklace a wide berth. Emily knelt and scooped the pennies into it. The rough metallic hot and cold of them on her hands again hurt her heart more than handing them over in the first place. She clicked the box shut and handed it to the Nocturne. As the pale hand touched it, Emily gripped on to the other end.

"And now you have to do your part."

"Of course, I have no choice, I told you this."

"Okay." Emily released the box and stood back. "I want to take my mom and dad home."

"And you shall." One tiny smile. "Once I've finished with them."

"WHAT?"

"When your mother has completed the task I need her for, then I shall release her and fulfill all the other requirements of the boon." The tiny smile widened. "I shall keep your father locked in a dungeon in the meantime to ensure your mother's cooperation."

Emily slipped under icy water.

"But you said you'd let them go."

"And I will. Right after she's done what I need her to do."

"But that's not what we agreed!"

"That is EXACTLY what we agreed!" The Nocturne did not raise her voice, but it swelled to fill the room and the chandeliers trembled. "This was a bargain, made in accordance with Ancient Law. Did you say anything of times or dates? Did you name your days? NO. The pennies for your parents and your safe conduct from me, and so shall it be."

She turned to go, and Emily shrieked at her.

"But I didn't know I needed to say that stuff! It's not fair!"

The Nocturne turned back, face empty of pity or a trace of humanity now.

"Fair? When has ignorance ever been an excuse in this world or yours?" Her hand stroked the silver box. "Ask the people your empire conquered, whose music was silenced, if they were given leave for lack of knowledge, or the chance to learn."

"But, but . . ."

Emily's throat was so full of fear and regret she was choking on it. The Nocturne's gaze held no more emotion than if Emily had been an insect.

"Is it fair I should be trapped in here, starving and fading away, forced to subsist on smuggled scraps, whilst out there a feast awaits me? Is that fair? Is it?"

As she mentioned scraps, her eyes had jumped to the gramophone.

"Burke, bring the music. One of the new ones. I have need."

The butler spidered over to the gramophone and cranked the handle, then heaved it up into his arms, groaning as he did, and moved to stand behind his mistress. The unexpected lyrics of "Anarchy in the UK" echoed from the horn and the sound of electric guitars rattled around the ballroom, and the Nocturne threw her head back in exultation. All the edges of her were lined with a crackling electric charge, and she had started to glow. The thick gray streaks in the Nocturne's hair first shrank then turned to glossy black. The Nocturne opened eyes that now blazed with light.

"I will live like this no more. Ursus, we have both the coins and a trickster to handle them. Start the plan. Unleash chaos, then get them to the Great Working. I will neutralize the guard and force the nag to place them as required." She smiled in cold triumph. "With the coins to warp the charm, the chimes will ring out, and I can twist the music to do my bidding. The Great Working will work for me alone."

Humming under her breath, she walked toward the door, the Bear beside her, and the staggering butler and gramophone following behind.

Emily sobbed her pain.

"You, you promised it wouldn't harm the Great Working! You lied!"

The blazing eyes were turned on her once more.

"I tell no lies, child. I will not harm the Great Working. Instead, I shall rip it free from this prison, wrap it around me and mine as a cloak of midnight, and walk back into your age with all my magic intact."

"And Bear will hunt in new dark!" said the Bear.

The Nocturne smiled at him, the indulgent mother of a terrifying, furry child.

"Yes, you shall. We shall all be free to feast again."

Emily was drowning now, with no way to claw back up to the surface.

"But, but, what about the Midnight Hour, the people here?"

"They shall have no choice but to come into the other world, as I had *no choice* to come to this one when your mother trapped me." She glared at Emily.

"But this is a sanctuary! Everything's changed; they can't survive out there without magic!" She was begging now.

"I hunger, and so I will feed. Nothing else matters."

Her expression was terrible beyond words, filled with nothing but her own awful need. She was at the door now but turned back.

"Nothing . . . except perhaps repaying your mother's old insult to my honor. I promised not to do you harm, and I will not, but . . ." Her bony finger wagged again. ". . . your boon did not bind any other nor ask me to. The details are very important, remember."

The Bear opened the door and he and the Nocturne went through without looking back.

Your boon did not bind any other, what did she mean?

A shape emerged from the shadows in the hallway. The part-squashed, part-torn, and all-terrifying shape of Lord Stabville-Chest lurched in, slamming the door shut behind him. His evening suit and opera cape were ripped beyond repair, and one of his red eyes was missing, but the remains of his face split open to reveal he still had all his teeth.

"I haven't drunk fresh blood in over a century and a half. Guess what I'm going to do to you, little nag?"

CHAPTER 19

Peregrine lurched toward her, all grace gone but still cat-quick. Fear moved Emily's feet before her brain caught up. She darted away, throwing the chairs between them as the hungry vampire hurtled after her. The fire burned hot at her back, and the wrecked windows hung open behind Peregrine. Why hadn't she gone that way? The vampire didn't bother to dodge around, but smashed one of the chairs out of the way with a flick of his arm. It flew across the room and exploded into matchsticks on the wall. He was MUCH stronger than he looked. Emily hovered behind the other chair. There was nowhere to run.

"You! You have *no* respect for the Dead!" he snarled, and a line of horrible bloody dribble went all down the front of his already ruined shirt. "You made me look stupid in front of her."

"You didn't need much help." It was out of her gob before she could stop it. Why, oh why?

Peregrine howled in outrage and leapt, knocking the remaining chair aside and grabbing her as she tried to duck away. He was all bone and nails and teeth, and his claws sank through her jacket and into her arm. She shrieked as he pulled her toward him. His one remaining eye glowed red, and his teeth were longer than ever, jutting out of his smashed face, shards of yellowed bone. He could barely talk past them, but one word came out.

"HUNGRY!"

He drew his head back and darted forward at her neck, a cobra striking. She didn't have time to scream. All of a sudden the same odd sensation of liquidness bloomed in her chest, then spread in a flash to the rest of her body, from the top of her head to the tips of her toes. There was a horrid squashing and bending sensation, then she was shrinking and falling out of his grip. She rolled and kicked out with her back legs and pushed away, and then all four of her feet hit the floor, and she was off away under the chaise longue, her long ears brushing it as her powerful back legs pushed her forward in a bounding run, speeding up and out. The soft fur of her paws slid a bit on the polished wooden floor, and she had to carve a wide turning circle but, as the vampire howled with rage behind her she straightened out and sped forward across the floor, out through the splintered windows and onto the rhino lawn.

As she hit the night air, her little nose twitched and everything around her flooded in. The grass, the graves, the turn of the wind, and the rotting stink of a hungry and desperate vampire sprinting after her. Her big oval eyes, set on either side of her head, spotted the thickest set of bushes across the lawn, and she was off, long ears flattened, and paws gaining perfect grip on the grass, letting her reach immense speed as she bounded across, dodging between the stationary rhino and going so fast all four of her paws left the ground at the same time as she ran. She flowed and leapt and flew, leaving the anguished vampire far behind, and hurtled into the bushes without slowing down. Her eyes, ears, and whiskers telling her left, right, duck, left, left, dodge, and she cannoned through and out the other side into a field. She found a fox-track by the hedgeline, sniffed to be sure it hadn't been used, then ran up it, glorying in her perfect form and the grass and fields, sensing everything around her. The moonlight silvered her tawny back and black-tipped ears, and she kicked for joy, first back legs then front, boxing at the air. She was free and running, and nothing could touch her. She ran for miles and miles, never tiring, until she reached a stone wall that smelled safe, and hopped over it into the corner of an old walled garden, untouched for years, with a fine clump of clover inside. She stopped, sniffed, and listened for danger. Finding none, she buried her head and chewed her fill. Once she was full, she turned around and around in the longer grass, flattening it down to form a space perfect for her body, and settled down to rest.

A little while later there was an unusual noise, like perhaps that of a compressed spring firing a practical joke paper snake out of an opened jar. Emily erupted up out of the hare's form in the grass, and leapt into the air.

"WHAT THE FLIPPING HECK WAS THAT?" she screamed, then spat out the remaining grass.

She stood shivering with shock, hands clutched to her chest, trying to get used to having both eyes back on the front of her head. She grabbed at her ears, and then patted herself all over: head, yes, feet, yes, butt, yes but no tail, oh thank goodness. All limbs present and correct and the right shape. All her clothes were there, too, but she'd lost her bag when she'd fled from Peregrine, and . . .

"HOG!"

She rummaged in her coat pocket and produced a spherical Hog. He had rolled up into a defensive ball and rocked on her palm, tucked into himself and all abristle with spikes.

"Hoggins, are you okay?"

There was a twitch and he unfolded very gradually. As his nose and little face were revealed, he gave her a wide-eyed look of outrage, and turned to face away from her with a huff.

"Oh, Hog, I'm sorry, I don't know what happened. Where did you go? I mean I was a big rabbity thing or something. They don't even have pockets."

The Hog remained facing the other way. Sulking was one of Emily's expert subjects, and the Hog had got a bad case of it.

"Oh dear. Here, let me find you a treat."

She walked up among the overgrown vegetable beds until she spotted a juicy slug. She winced but picked it up, then dangled its horrible slimy body over her palm.

"Hog?"

There was a snuffling sound and he inched back around to face her. He was still wrinkled up with annoyance.

"Here." She dropped the slug on her palm, and he bit it before it could slime away. Terrible slurping and crunching noises ensued. It was all disgusting, but his face uncreased a bit.

"I'm very sorry, and once I figure out what just happened, I won't let it happen to you again, okay?"

He didn't look up from his chewing, but shook his wiggly butt and twitched his nose, and that was that, sulk over. She slid him and the half-eaten slug back into her pocket. Her mom was going to want to wash that when she got it back. Her mom . . .

The awful disaster that had just unfolded washed over her as an icy wave. She'd ruined everything, and didn't even have the pennies now. What was that terrifying woman going to do with her mom and dad? With the Midnight Hour? Emily dropped down into the damp grass and sat with her back against a tumbledown shed. A shed . . . the sudden pulse of loss knotted her stomach. It had been an often embarrassing, boring, little life, and yet now, she'd have given anything to be sitting on her own bed with a book, struggling to read over the hammering sounds and blasting punk, or trying to watch TV over the rumble of her dad snoring on the settee. Little things she'd thought were glass she now could see were diamonds.

She'd been sitting there for a long while, staring into space, when a loud cough made her jump and bang her head against the plank behind. It wasn't a real cough, but one of those coughs someone does when they're trying to get your attention.

"Ah-hurrmm."

The cough was coming from a horse standing just beyond the low wall at the bottom of the garden.

In fact, it was *the* horse–the black stallion that had saved her from the Bear. It had the white blaze at the top of its mane and red eyes. It coughed once more, then, sure it had gotten her attention, it walked behind a tree and, although it wasn't a very big tree, didn't come back out the other side. There was a distinct whooshing sound, and what did come out the other side was a tall, lean man in a threadbare black suit, with a flat cap and a red scarf. There was a distinct white streak in the thick black hair poking out from beneath the cap. He turned and leaned on the wall and pulled a dirty bit of rolled-up paper from behind his ear. He lit it with a match he struck on the stone in front of him and filled the air between them with foul-smelling smoke.

"Well now, tough woman to find, you are."

That voice! It was the same Irish voice and the same man who'd come to her front door at the very start of all this. He wasn't from the truancy board at all. He was . . .

"A Pooka! You're a Pooka!"

"Oh well, ten out of ten. There's nothing wrong with yer observation skills at least." He dragged again on the horrid roll-up. "Although the rest of yer brain-functioning is still in question. Are ye just trying to get killed or what? I can't be runnin' 'round savin' ye all the time, I've important business of me own."

"You, you didn't save me. I did. I . . . I turned into something."

He waved his hand.

"Ah, I was just about to spring into action there, when ye finally pulled yer finger out and acted the true Pooka. I thought ye'd never get 'round to it."

"What?"

She hurled herself to her feet, then had to clutch at the shed as a wave of dizziness overwhelmed her.

"I, oh, I feel wonky."

"Ah, that's the change. Is that yer first one? It's tricksy until ye've practiced. I normally go for a pint and some peanuts after a long one. Cushions the system." He craned his neck and looked around. "Speaking of which, did ye happen to spot a pub anywhere 'round here?"

"But, what happened?" Emily groped for the right words. "Where did the rest of me go?"

"Ah, it all goes up." He pointed vaguely at the air above his head. "Then it all comes down again. Best not to worry about it. Bound to leave ye feeling a bit peaky, though. Do you want a ciggie?"

"What? No! Smoking's disgusting."

"More for me, then."

"Why did you call me a Pooka?"

He shook his head.

"Well, the brains don't run in the family, do they?"

She slumped back against the shed.

"I can't handle any more freaky stuff."

He frowned and hurdled the wall, landing smartly on the balls of his feet and strolling over to take a seat on an old upside-down bucket.

"Freaky stuff is a strong family tradition, so it is. Man and boy, I've been up to all sorts, barking hymns at priests, going down chimneys . . ."

Barking? A vision of a big black, whistling dog with a white streak came back into focus.

"Wait, were you that dog, too? You were, weren't you? Who are you and why are you following me?"

He brightened at that and jumped off the bucket, spun on his heels, sticking both thumbs in the pockets of the vest, and straightening up with a grin.

"That's an easy one." He whipped his cap off and bowed in front of her. "I am yer uncle, Patrick Connolly, at yer service, and I'm keeping an eye on yer, all official-like, as deputized by yer ma."

CHAPTER 20

Pat looked up from his bow to where Emily sat silent, ashen faced and open mouthed.

"Who's my sister, which is why I'm yer unc–"

"I know what an uncle is! My mom doesn't have a brother!" she shouted.

He straightened up and replaced his cap.

"Well, that's a very hurtful thing to hear of me own flesh and blood," he said and clutched his heart.

Emily stamped her foot.

"Stop saying that! You're not . . ."

But he was. He was lanky where her mom was short, but they had the same cheekbones, and long nose, and way of looking at you with their head on one side. He was doing it right now, in fact. The black hair tumbling over his piercing green eyes from beneath his battered cap was the final clue. Her mom's hair hadn't been a normal color in years, but it was jet-black underneath when her roots showed through, and her eyes were the same emerald green: electric, alive, and full of mischief. Pat's eyes twinkled just the same as he winked at her.

"Oh god, you are, aren't you?"

"Oh yes."

"But you're a Pooka?"

"Obviously."

"So, Mom's a . . ."

"Yeeees," he said, making a winding gesture with his finger. *Go on . . .*

"So, does that mean, I'm . . . I'm a Pooka, too?"

"Finally!"

He kicked a couple of jig steps in celebration, then slouched back against the wall. He appeared to have an aversion to standing up straight.

"But what, why? HOW?"

"Well, when a mammy and a daddy love each other very much, sometimes they—"

"No, stop!" she screamed. "Not that. I mean, how, why? Why didn't she tell me?"

He shifted from foot to foot and wouldn't meet her eye.

"Well, things haven't been exactly grand between yer ma and the Connolly clan after her great disgrace, and then her eloping out the Hour an' all." He shrugged. "An' you can't truly be a Pooka out there, not without magic. Perhaps she just . . ." He shrugged again.

"What? *Forgot!*" Emily wanted to throw up and it wasn't just from her transformation.

"Was waiting until youse was more grown up."

"Into what? A pony!"

"Nah, horses take practice. Yer miles off yet." Pat took a long drag on his horrible roll-up and puffed a smoke ring. "Anyways, I'm here now to tell ye all about it. Think of me as a mental figure."

"As a what?"

He frowned.

"*Mentor*, that's the one. Ask me anything."

Emily whacked herself on the head with her own clenched fist. How, how, how was this her life?

"Why are you here?"

He grinned.

"That's easy. Yer ma popped in on me a wee while ago, dearly beloved to her as I am, and regaled me with a list of the offal troubles she was having, pursued by villainous types and such, and I, without hesitation, volunteered my services to take a message in person to the Daylight realm, and keep an eye on my poor sweet niece, in the face of the dreadful forces of darkness." He nodded, green eyes shimmering and trustworthy. "It was, in fact, fierce brave of me, and she was very grateful."

There was a way to tell when Pat was lying; his lips would move.

"That's . . . that's not true at all, is it?"

"Ye doubt the word of yer recently discovered, long-abandoned uncle of yer blood? I'm shocked." He clutched his heart. Again.

"Yes, I flippin' do! You, you can't walk straight! You're a proper Pooka, and that means you're a bad lot. Not like Mom!"

"Ah, ye've heard of her disgrace, then?" He grimaced.

"What flippin' disgrace? Do you mean running off with Dad?" Her brain was whirling so fast there was every chance the top of her head would come off.

"What, eloping? Oh no, that's a family tradition. No, it was the other business." He sighed. "It was brutal for the clan to have to cope with, it was."

"If you don't tell me what you mean, I swear I'll . . ."

He held a hand up to placate her.

"I mean, the greatest thief and trickster the Connolly's ever had, joining the Library and fighting for the common good. The shame of it." He closed his eyes at the memory. "It was the upset over it all that finished Great-Auntie Aoife off, everybody says so."

"Wait, Mom being a hero is a disgrace?" said Emily.

"We're Pooka, girl! It's a proud tradition. We're tricksters and rogues, beasts of ill-omen. We don't help people! The very thought of it."

He mopped his forehead with a grubby spotted handkerchief.

"So why are you helping me, then? And don't lie."

"Well, there's plenty of the clan'd deny ever having met our Maeve, of course, but we was always close, and so I had to step up when she asked."

She folded her arms across her chest, and just glared at him.

"It's true!" His eyes were wide with innocence. "She asked me to send a message to yer da and keep an eye on ye. Even gave me her shadow key to get in and out." He rummaged in his pockets to show her.

"And . . ." She tapped her foot.

He leaned in close and spoke in a hushed whisper.

"And she maybe has a lot of evidence of things she claims I've done, that I'd rather not come out. Not that any of it's true, but y'know. She's an evil mare when the mood takes her."

He patted her shoulder.

"But I mainly did it out the decency of me heart."

She smacked his hand away.

"You were blackmailed! You don't care!"

He gave her full puppy eyes.

"I do! A bit. If it's not going to interfere. I've got the racing later, y'know."

Emily stamped off to fume, but then came straight back.

"Why didn't you just say who you were when you came to the house? Why? I'd have . . ." She trailed off, not quite sure what she would have done.

"Did I not? Really?"

"No!"

"Hmm. I thought I was very clear. I had a filthy head on me, though." Pat winced in recollection. "Daylight and brandy's a fierce combination."

Emily wondered if it was possible to spontaneously combust just from sheer annoyance.

"Argh, you're infuriating! What was this message you said about? You never gave us a message."

"Ahhh . . ." He paused. "Did I say a message? I don't remember that."

"Yes!"

"Ah, I can see where ye're getting confused." He smiled and waved his finger. "There may, in fact, have been a message, and yer ma asked a man, another man, to take it to yer da, but he may well have been delayed."

"Was that other man also you by any chance?" said Emily.

"I really couldn't say, it'd break a family confidence."

"Was the delay a pub?"

"I don't think we should get bogged down in the details here. Let's just say mistakes were made and we've all learnt from them." Pat nodded sagely.

Emily grabbed his jacket lapels.

"What. Was. The. Message?" she ground out from between clenched teeth.

"Well, it might have been something about there being a plot to break the Hour with some unlucky pennies, the need to hide them and ye away so you definitely wouldn't end up in here, and a place for yer da to meet her while she spied on the Nocturne." He mumbled and didn't meet her eye.

"You, you're unbelievable! If you'd have delivered the message straight away like she asked you to, my dad would have known where to go, and I wouldn't be here, and I'd still have the coins and . . . this is all your fault, you *eejit*!"

"That could actually be the family motto," he mused.

A white-hot fury burned through her.

"Right, that's it. You're going to make this right. We're going to get my mom and dad and stop the Nocturne!"

"Whoa there!" He held both hands out. "She's a rum sort. We'd be better going for a quiet pint until it all blows over."

"She's got your sister and she's trying to blow the whole Midnight Hour up! You're going to help me."

"Am I, now?" He folded his arms and grinned a fox's grin. "Maeve's a big girl. She'll be fine, and I've got a very pressing schedule vis-à-vis my availability for heroics."

"You're going to help me or I'm going to get Mom's evidence folder out and report you! I've got friends in the Watch now." Or she used to, anyway.

Pat had to scratch an itch he'd developed under his cap, but most of the grin was still there.

"Yer bluffing."

"Am I? Oh, and Pat." She lowered her voice so he had to lean in. "Even if I am, and you don't help me, what's my mom going to say when she finds out what you did?"

He went pale.

"She is brutal when roused."

"Yes, she is."

She let him picture it, then said, "Me now, or her later. What's it to be?"

He grinned, and it was sunlight on a winter's day.

"Ah, you're a chip off the old block and no mistake. Textbook ominous threats. We'll make a proper Pooka of you yet. Okay, I'm in. What's it to be?"

"We're going straight to the Night Watch!"

"WHAT?"

It took her a while to calm Pat down. He had definite views about, what he termed, "the guard." She had to explain that she just needed to get to the main station. Once she told them about the Library and the Nocturne, and what was going on, they'd have to help her. Right?

"Right, well, I don't like it, but I promised I'd keep ye safe, and there's not much safer than the guard, I suppose." He scowled at the thought. "We're going in the back way, though. I've got me pride. Can ye change?"

"What, shape?" She rubbed at the little space between her collarbones. "I don't know how I did it the first time, and I still feel sick."

"Well, on this one occasion, ye being family and all, I'll give ye a lift. Ye best not be telling anybody."

He stared at her, tapping his foot with impatience.

"What?"

"Well, y'know." He flapped his hands at her, waving her away. "Turn around. It's not polite to watch a man change."

She turned around and from behind came the springy whooshing noise of air being pushed out of the way, followed by a distinctive whinny. She turned back and the black stallion stood there, proud and tall, with a white blaze in the forelock of its black mane. It still had the extinguished remains of the dirty, hand-rolled cigarette hanging from its lips. A big pink tongue came out and slurped it inside its mouth, and the horse began to chew. It moved closer to the wall and tossed its head at Emily.

After a series of false starts, she managed to step up and throw herself onto the broad, warm back and rocked there, uncertain. She clenched her knees tight and leaned forward to grab a handful of mane. The stallion took two gentle paces and then rocketed off at enormous speed, leaving only her scream behind.

After a long, sweaty, terrifying ride, Pat pulled up on a quiet street in St. James, by a large gate made of iron railings set into a stone wall. The wall was covered with a vivid purple climbing vine that hissed as they got near. Emily slid off and dug her knuckles into her cramped thighs.

"Never again."

There was a whoosh behind her, and Pat walked back into view, rubbing at his lower back.

"Too right," he said. "Ye need to lay off the cakes."

"Oi!"

He'd walked over to the gate and was cagily peering

through the bars. There was a lot of grass and some trees in the fog. The Hog was squirming in her pocket. He probably wanted the bathroom, but she'd have to let him out later.

"Okey-cokey, here we go," said Pat. "Ye go through the gate, across the lawn, and into the station the back way."

Emily peered into the murk.

"Where's the station?"

"Ah, way in there. That's why they call it Scotland Yard, 'cause of all this grass out the back. Hop out the moonlight fer a second." Something glinted shiny-black in his hand.

"What's that?"

"It's yer ma's shadow key. Ye have to use the shadow, not the key, and it'll open pretty much any door. Very useful."

He twisted himself out of the light, angled the black key over the lock, and the shadow danced across the gate and into the keyhole. A click of tumblers and it was open. Pat pulled the gate wide and waved her through.

"Right, ye pop in, and I'll wait here." He pulled his collar up high to cover his face. "There's a number of pressing reasons why I shouldn't go into a guard station."

She walked through, and he leaned in the gateway.

"Okay. Thank you, Pat."

"Uncle Pat." He smiled at her, gentler than his normal grin.

"Thank you, Uncle Pat." She grinned now. "Yup, still

sounds weird. Look, will you promise to wait? I've got a lot of questions about, what do you even call it? Pooka-ing?"

"Ah, it's a glorious life, the best of all. Wild and free. I'll teach ye everything."

A thrill of excitement tingled through her. If they got through this, then perhaps there *was* something here for her. A wild life full of magic and adventure. Something more than miserable school or boring, gray London. Wait. Boring, gray London . . . Since she'd stepped through the gate, something had been nagging at her. The light had changed from silver to a drab orange, and the air was different. There was less sewer in it and more car exhaust. Behind her, where she was sure she'd have seen it from the gate was a . . .

"Hang on, that's a streetlamp. This is my world!"

In the background now, she could hear the bongs echo across London, the wrong London.

A clunk and click from across the pavement. Pat had shut the gate behind her. He spoke to her through the bars.

"First lesson then. Never trust a Pooka."

"What are you doing?" she blurted. "I've got to get help."

"Well, here's the thing. I promised me sister, on silver and rowan, that I'd keep ye safe, and look, now yer safe and far away from harm."

Emily grabbed the bars of the gate, but he held it shut. Their faces were so close together the tobacco on his breath soured the air. The bongs were still ringing out, the bells that could never sound in the Midnight Hour.

"No, no, you can't! That woman's got Mom and Dad. She's going to do something dreadful to your whole world!"

Silver moonlight shone behind him as he shrugged.

"I'm sure it'll all be fine. It usually is."

"What if it's not?"

He gave her a sad half smile, winked once, then, as the twelfth and last bong rang out, he vanished. The moonlight disappeared and there was just an empty pavement tinted orange by streetlights. It was twelve o'clock exactly back home, and Emily was locked out of the Midnight Hour.

CHAPTER 21

Getting home was a nightmare. First Emily had to get someone to let her out of the private gardens she was locked into. There was a nasty moment when the police were going to be called by the angry custodian, but she managed to convince him she was part of the Hedgehog Rescue Team and was dealing with a serious case of Bolivian fleas. After that, he gave her a wide berth and let her walk out, carrying the offending Hog as if he were radioactive. Then she got a horrid series of night buses, which were at least less scary than in the Midnight Hour. No one on them had fangs or anything.

She sat, exhausted, head resting against a window full of lights and her own reflection. Neither of them looked right anymore. Normal was all she'd wanted to get back to but now, with its bright lights, noise, and smells, normal was as alien as the Hour ever had been. Her hand reached to the coins for comfort, but they were gone, and guilt hung around her neck in their place.

It was the early hours of the morning when she got back to the house. At least she didn't need to find her keys as someone had helpfully pulled the back door off its hinges. Inside was all ripped up, with every drawer and cupboard emptied out, and rents clawed in the sofas and beds. Someone very big and very angry had searched it for a magic necklace while she was away. She propped the door shut with a chair and picked her way upstairs through the fluff and wreckage without tidying a single thing. In her devastated room, the black glass hares lay shattered on the floor, their endless chase come to a violent end. She found Feesh the crocodile, who was thankfully safe and well, made a nest from her quilt and blankets, and passed out.

She woke up mid-afternoon the next day to something bright on her face. Daylight; she'd forgotten that. The sprawling damage surrounding her made her want to pull the covers back over her head. However, she was sure the Hog was hungry, and after all her sweaty, terrifying adventures, she totally needed a shower. She tiptoed her way through the broken glass of the poor Abbits to grab a towel and headed to the bathroom.

Half an hour later, she sat on the one remaining chair in the kitchen with the towel wrapped around her head and fresh underwear on. Fresh underwear was well known for making everything better, but she wasn't sure if it was going to work today.

She turned stale bread into toast and, to make space to eat it, scraped some of the smashed plates off the table and into the bin. What was the matter with her? She was all slow and confused. There was a great big clawing pool of panic underneath the slow progress she was making through the day, but she was disconnected from it. The endless night of the other world was already becoming a dream. She was back in her world, which was what she'd wanted, but now she just wished she could curl up into a ball and dream her way back to the other one. If only she knew how the dreamlings did it.

The Hog had eaten his cat food and was already asleep in his box in the corner. His little snores became the snores of all the other sickly hogs she'd seen her mom looking after right here at this table, and water began to flow from her eyes. She cried thick tears, cried after holding it in the whole time she'd been in the Midnight Hour, cried until it dripped from her chin and onto her toast. The great big whirling mass of panic started to claw its way out. Everything was ruined and it was completely her fault. She'd lost the bad pennies, and the key to get back in, her mom and dad were prisoners, and that dreadful woman was going to take the magic and protection of the Midnight Hour for herself and break the whole other world in the process. She'd promised Tarkus his family would be okay, but instead their safe haven would rupture, and they'd be cast back out into the Daylight realm. She'd just been scared and wanted to make things normal, and now they'd never be normal again.

Nothing about her life made sense. Her parents were strangers, and she . . . she wasn't human. She collapsed on the table, hands fisted on either side of her head. Everything was awful, and she was locked out of the Midnight Hour, unable to do anything to help.

She stayed that way for a long time, wracked with sobs. Eventually, her towel fell off and she sat up. Her toast was miserably soggy, and some of it had stuck to her face. She wiped herself clean with the towel, then blew her nose with it, too. After all, there's only so long you can sit and wallow for, and then you just have to get on with it. This was another one of her mom's sayings. In fact, she had to admit a lot of the bits of advice she told herself came from her mom. "Never be knowingly under-snacked. Big boots are best. Biscuits make everything better." All of the good ones. So, instead of continuing to have a massive meltdown, she grabbed some biscuits and a pad and pen, and sat down on the one remaining sofa cushion to try her mom's other little gem—"When in doubt, make a list."

First, she made a list of problems:

Mom and Dad prisoners

Terrifying magical musical lady

Foolishly traded coins that could end a world

Possible end of world

Locked out of Midnight Hour due to lost key (and eejit uncle)

A very angry friend (or whatever he is), Tarkus

Then she made another column and listed her assets. She had to chew the end of her pen over this one, and it was still a much shorter list. It included:

The Hog (obvs)

A friend in the post office

An ally(?) in the Library

Being a magical Pooka person (but not in this world)

That one still gave her the willies, but it needed to go on the list.

This was all taking so long, and the panic started to pinch again. She ran her pen down all the items on the list. Yup, that was it. How was any of this going to help? There had to be something in there somewhere. There just had to be. She considered making one of those big work-it-all-out things, with pins and different colored string and photos, that you see on the wall in TV shows, but as she didn't have any string or photos, it was a bit of a waste of time.

It was useless, she'd lost all the things from the Midnight Hour with her bag. The all-important key, the Library card, the Night Post badge—hang on, that wasn't everything, was it? There was something else, but she just hadn't known what they were before. Eejit!

She winced at the destruction in her dad's tiny office. The desk had been ransacked but, under a pile of *Composters' Weekly*, there they were. The big envelope full of stamps, most of them black and beautiful, but two of them huge, bloodred, and shiny. Bloody Marys—extra-special delivery stamps. All you needed was a true name and they'd be delivered immediately anywhere, in either world, Tarkus had said. She bit her knuckle to help her think. Maybe, just maybe, she had a plan. Having added the stamps to her list of assets, she wrote ideas down, drawing lines between the two columns. Many of those lines sprang from the word "stamps." It started to look like a work-it-all-out wall on the TV after all.

"Ha!" she said. "I'm a genius."

The Hog cracked one eye open, then shook his head and went back to sleep.

After that the day passed in a whirl of activity. She got her dad's battered old computer going and looked some things up to confirm her suspicions. She started with the invention of the gramophone, then moved on to music websites, muttering to herself as she did.

"Oh, you sneaky cow."

Then she researched diagrams of clockwork, relating to one big clock in particular, and found out something *very* interesting about how the timing was fine-tuned. Once again, she had cause to mutter about sneaky cows.

Curiosity satisfied, she dug out two massive cardboard boxes that were folded flat in her mom's crowded studio and reassembled them, wrapping all the seams and corners in thick silver gaffer tape from her mom's toolbox. When they were sturdy enough, she moved them into the hall and then went upstairs.

She took a long hard look at her many shelves and piles of books, shrugged, and started to grab random armfuls, cart them downstairs, and drop them into one of the boxes. It was slow going, as she kept flipping through the books she was meant to be packing into the box. She just couldn't help it. After losing ten whole minutes in *A Wrinkle in Time*, she had to be strict with herself. Picking them up upside down helped.

She was sweating by the time she was done but, with careful stacking, she had filled the one box and taped it shut. She lined the other box with her quilt and padded it with cushions. She punched a number of holes in the sides with a screwdriver, then stood back to survey her work. She frowned, then grabbed a marker and wrote, "This way up!" with a series of arrows on each side of the box. Satisfied, she headed to the kitchen and made a packed lunch from what was left in the cupboards. She'd always been partial to a chip sammie, anyway.

It was dark now. Glancing at the clock, Emily wrote out two letters in her best handwriting and put them both in their own envelopes. She wrote a name she partly shared on one, then folded it in half and tucked it inside the other, along with one of the vast red stamps. She sealed the envelope, put a black stamp on it, then addressed it to a friend in a building in St. Martin's Le Grand that no longer existed. That done, she wrote an address in Bloomsbury that was also a name onto the box of books. She plastered it with all the remaining black stamps, and gagged at the taste of the glue. What did they make that out of? To finish off, she wrote a single true name onto the other box, the one with all the padding in it, and slapped the remaining red stamp on top.

She slipped her mom's bomber jacket back on and grabbed the packed lunch, some water, the gaffer tape, and a flashlight. She popped the Hog back in her pocket, clambered into the padded box, and pulled the lid shut. She sat there for a minute, cursed, and got back out. Every time! She ran to the downstairs bathroom for an emergency pee, popped the latch on the front door, then jumped back in. She turned her flashlight on and put one final strip of the tape across the inside of the lid.

"Well, Hoggins, here goes nothing."

After that she sat in her box and waited for midnight.

She started awake to the sound of the first chimes drifting across the Thames. There were some difficult seconds as the fourth quarter chimes rang out and nothing happened, but then, with the first bong, came the squeak of ill-oiled brakes, and the click of the gate. Of course, it wasn't midnight until the big bell sang.

"Now then, whatever's all this?" The front door squeaked open as the gruff voice spoke. "Oh gawd, would you look at that lot! Where's blinkin' Alan when you need him, eh?"

Somebody came in the house, and there was a rustle as the letter was picked up. "Easy one. Goin' to see her at the depot."

Her box lurched as somebody picked one end up. She had to brace herself against the sides to stop from sliding.

"Strike a bloomin' light, that's heavy." More shuffling, then a groan of outrage as the weight of the book box was tested. "Won't no one think of poor old Jonesy's back? Gawd, I'll need a truss after this."

There were more footsteps, then some rattling and dinging

as the man searched for something on his bike. The midnight bongs were ringing out their count across the river. Emily felt sick. How long was this going to take? If the bongs finished, midnight would be over and surely that meant they'd be stuck outside?

"Where's that bloomin' umbrella?"

There was the click of an umbrella opening, and then all the hair on her arms stood up and her flashlight made a fizzing noise as the bulb inside it popped. The final bongs that had been ringing outside slowed to a long, persistent note. She was inside the little shadow of magic cast by a Night Shade and time had stopped.

"That's better," said Jonesy's voice, but it was even gruffer and deeper now, and when he gripped the box, he lifted it with a smooth strength, without a moan or a groan. She wondered what Jonesy was, then remembered it was rude to ask.

"Alley-oop and in the bag."

And then Emily was sideways and tumbling, a going-through-a-vacuum-cleaner suction tugged at her brain, and it all went spinny and stomach-churny, and she was . . . posted.

CHAPTER 22

Emily blinked back into reality as the box was clunked down on a hard surface. It hurt her butt, despite the layers of quilt and pillow, but she managed not to squeak. She was all bundled up and a bit upside down in one corner of the box, and had sat on her chip sandwiches.

"Here, love, express delivery for ya to take."

That was Jonesy again. His heavy footsteps echoed, and he sounded very large indeed. Did that mean she was in the Midnight Hour? She tried to shift herself without making a noise, and pressed her eye to one of the air holes. She couldn't see a thing.

"Another? Whoooo-ever is sending these? None in a decade, and twoooo this week!"

That voice.

"S'like omnibuses, innit? See ya later, feathers."

"Goodbye, Mr. Jones. Give my best to the goats."

Jonesy clumped away, and a soft, almost soundless step came close to the box.

"How very unusual."

There was a whisper of movement, then a huge eye was pressed to the same hole Emily's was, and she had to jam a hand in her mouth not to scream.

"Oh-hoo! I see." The eye moved away. "Of course, the post must never be used for transporting people. A good job it isn't, I think."

The softest of touches on the top of the box, as feathered fingers ran over it, then a smooth sensation of movement, and the box was lifted without any tipping, tilting, or groaning.

"Hold tight once more then, featherling."

Then came the vacuum-cleaner effect again and Emily was plunged back into the postbag.

She came back to herself this time, as a bell jangled and a door rattled shut.

"Night Post, express delivery!"

"What's all that?" snarled a deep voice. "We're shutting this station in the hemergency. You'll have to come back."

Emily was sliding around as the parcel moved with the owl-lady who flowed on dancer's feet.

"I seek a Tarkus Poswa."

"Ain't nobody called that here."

"Of course there is, or the stamp wouldn't have brought us here."

A chair screeched back, and heavy feet hit the floor.

"I said there ain't no Possum here. Now get out, we're in a state of hemergency!"

Emily's heart sank, but then . . .

"Uhmm, Sarge?"

"What is it, Postlewhite? You're supposed to be getting them drains unblocked, ain't you?"

"Working on it, Sarge. It's just, I think that's for me."

"WHAT?" the Sarge roared. Emily decided she didn't like him very much at all.

"It's an . . . erm . . . common misspelling of my name." Even Tarkus didn't sound convinced by this.

"Reeeeally?" said the Sarge.

"Erm, yes," said Tarkus.

"And that," shouted the Sarge, "is why I don't hold with all that readin' and writin'! You can't trust it. Now get it out of my sight, Possum."

"Let me help you with that, young man," said the owl-lady. "It's very heavy indeed."

"Oi," muttered Emily.

There was the sound of another door opening, then the package settled onto a hard surface.

"Here, a very important package. I'd open it privately if I were you." There was a flutter of feathers. "Oh, and young man—your real name is beau-ooh-tiful. It suits you."

There was nothing but a shuffling of shoes in response from Tarkus.

"Good luck, featherlings."

A swish and a swoosh and the sound of the door closing. There was silence, then Emily was pitched and rolled as Tarkus shook the box.

"Hey, careful!" she said.

There was a muffled squeak of surprise, then a scrabbling, a scratching, and she had to duck away as something sharp and pointy sliced along the tape. She squinted against the sudden radiance, the gas lamps were bright after the dark of the box. The brightness was blotted out by the face of a very, very angry ghûl.

"YOU!"

She unfolded herself from the pretzel shape she was in and creaked to her feet, her back aching. They were in a small side office, with little more than a desk, a chair, and a lot of big folders on shelves. There was a harsh, peppery scent in the air, abrasive to the nose. That was a first in her rage-inducing career. She'd never made anybody *smell* angry before.

"Look—"

"What were you thinking? That's not my name here!" His yellow eyes glowed brighter than the gas lamps.

"I'm sorry! I didn't know if the stamp would work otherwise, and it doesn't matter." His face grew ever more thunderous but she pressed on. "There's some serious police stuff you need to know about. We've got to get help."

"No. No more of your nonsense. You are under arrest."

He was patting his pockets as he talked.

"For what?"

"Assaulting an officer! Ah ha!" He brandished bright silver handcuffs.

"You fell down a hole!"

His eyes glowed even brighter. Hopefully he wouldn't set his eyebrows on fire.

"Abandoning an officer, then! Handing over vital evidence." He advanced on her, handcuffs dangling. She edged around the side of the desk, away from him.

"The coins were mine, and you nearly strangled me with them!"

He paused at that. She spoke fast, keeping the desk in the way, just in case.

"Look, I didn't come here to argue. I came here to . . .

well." She looked at her feet. "I came here to say sorry to start with."

"Oh," he said.

"What?"

"Well, that's a surprise." His face was unreadable. "I didn't think you were a 'sorry' type of person."

"What's that meant to . . . ?" She stopped herself. "I suppose I'm not, normally. But I shouldn't have left you down the hole. Sorry.

"And," she said, before he could start. "I shouldn't have gone off with the coins, but you totally shouldn't have tried to snatch them, either."

He nodded, a tight little gesture.

"I, also, am sorry for that."

"Well, me too."

There was a brief silence between them. The background scent changed to something sweet and herbal, a leaf her mom might have cooked with once.

"You're still under arrest, of course."

"WHAT?"

"Ha! Your face!"

She hadn't heard him laugh before. It was dry and high and kind.

"Oh, very funny, Violet."

"Why are you here? What happened with the Nocturne?"

He put the handcuffs away in his pocket and sagged back on the desk. "I tried to tell the Sarge about it, but he won't listen because the city's in chaos right now."

"What do you mean?"

"The Angry Dead have rioted. They're demanding to leave the Hour. Idiots." His face was gaunt with tiredness. "There's been mayhem everywhere. We're run ragged, every officer is out on the streets, and they've called in the reserves."

"Then why are you still here?" she said.

The flame of his eyes glowed from under heavy brows as he glared at her.

"Because I am restricted to desk duties after losing both my official truncheon and an important prisoner, then being found in a *sewer.*"

"Ah. Look, I apologize, okay."

"Yes, you said. I'm still considering whether to accept it or not."

"I'm sure you'll see the funny side. In the meantime, there's some VERY important things you need to know."

He let out a long-suffering sigh.

"Go on."

"You're a what?"

"I know. It's all a shock to me, too. I mean, does that make me part rabbit or what?" She twitched her nose. "I don't even eat vegetables, let alone grass."

"Hare."

"I'm not eating that, either," she said.

"No, hare. Pooka can be hares, hounds, and horses." He shook his head with disapproval. "Why do you not know this? Heritage is important."

"I didn't know I had a flippin' heritage until I grew massive ears and legged it. It was . . ." She paused, unsure. ". . . it was weird and kinda cool, I suppose. But mainly weird. I mean, like, where did my pants go?"

"So you're a beast of ill-omen? Well, that explains why you can hold the pennies . . ." Tarkus leaned back in his seat with a scowl and folded his arms. ". . . and a great deal about my week so far."

"Enough moaning. Mistakes happened, we've all learned something." She flinched as Pat and his sad smile filled her head. "We need to do something. It's all a big plan. I've figured it out, I think." She tried not to gabble as she explained something that would have sounded like total nonsense to her a few days ago.

"She's bringing in new music from my world to power herself up. That's why she's not gone as wobbly as the Library." She slammed the desk with her hand. "I know why she needs my mom, too! She's going to get her to put the bad pennies onto the pendulum inside Big Ben."

"What? Why?" Tarkus rocked forward again, his hands slapping the desk as the chair shifted under him.

"Because the timing is set by–guess what–old coins!" She was proud of figuring this out. "I looked it up on the interne–a big library we have on my side. They use pennies on the pendulum to make tiny adjustments to keep it accurate. It sounds mad but it's true."

Tarquin's eyes went wide.

"So, the most important clock and spell in both worlds . . ." he said.

". . . only works because of an exact number of old coins," she finished for him. "Imagine what a whole lot of cursed pennies could do."

"But breaking the spell . . . that's madness."

"She isn't going to break it, though. She said she's going to get control of it and take all the magic with her so she can go into the Daylight realm. She's going to let all her nasties out with her, too."

Tarkus went a peculiar green color, and the sour fug of rotting leaves filled the small room.

"But without magic . . . if time moves again, the Midnight Hour will pop like a bubble! We'd all be plunged back into the Daylight realm!" His big yellow eyes brimmed with tears. "My family can't survive there anymore! They'd be hunted. Without magical protection, we'd never be safe again."

The hot shame from before returned threefold and left her feeling sick.

"Why? Why would she do this?" said Tarkus, face twisted with anguish.

"She wants the magic and the music all for herself, and she doesn't care what happens to anybody else." Emily shuddered at the memory of those eyes. "She looks fancy but she's just . . . all emptiness and hunger. She talks about wanting to be free, but I think she just wants the power."

Tarkus's lips moved as his mind raced.

"This would destroy my home, all our homes. We were meant to be safe here."

His eyes dipped from their usual golden yellow to a burnt bronze color.

"I don't know what it would do to your world, but . . . all of the Angry Dead released, her with the midnight spell? Nowhere would be safe."

Silence filled the space between them. Tarkus's eyes began to burn brighter.

"I won't see my family suffer again, nor anybody else's. I have to stop her."

"*I* have to stop her—it's all my fault," said Emily.

"I thought you just wanted to go home."

She flushed beet red.

"Yeah, well, I've had a chance to think about that. It's amazing how being a massive rabbit can—"

"Hare."

"Whatever, Trevor. How being a massive HARE can make you think about stuff." She looked straight into his yellow, fiery eyes. "I'm sorry I was a git. Let's stop her together and get my mom and dad back. And that's totally the last apology you're getting."

"Accepted, Miss Featherhaugh. What are we going to do?"

"I've got a bit of a plan. I've sent for help, because I'm not an idiot, but she's got the Bear and who knows what else. What about the Watch?"

Tarkus's face twisted in frustration.

"Sarge wouldn't listen. The only reason I haven't been dismissed yet is because of the uprising. There's not a Night Watch officer in London who isn't out on the stree . . ." He trailed off. "That's very convenient, isn't it?"

"This is the chaos she asked the Bear to make. Her plan is happening right now." Emily stood up, did a quick Hogcheck, and grabbed her squashed sandwich bag. She was ready. "We have to get to the Great Working."

He let out another heavy sigh and a faint aroma of rosemary, then stood up, too.

"As my official prisoner, I'm coming with you, of course. It's miles from here, though. I pray we get there in time."

Emily grinned. "We will; I wrote a letter asking a friend if I could borrow a bike."

CHAPTER 23

The bike was left out under a tarpaulin at the side of the Night Post building, just as she'd asked Japonica to do in the letter she'd sent. A note was stuck on the saddle.

Bike as requested. Will be using the Bloody Mary you sent to deliver the other letter in person. Excellent thinking. Thank you for your warning, but it is they who will need to be careful if they have imprisoned an employee of the Night Post. I will be taking Mr. Jones and his goats along.

I return your warning—Please be careful.

Your friend,

Japonica

She won the dispute about who was cycling after claiming

to be "postie by genetics!" although it had led to her having to explain genetics (quite badly) to a dubious Tarkus. Some pretty major technical difficulties were experienced with take-off (two crashes, one whole manticore in a fancy hat knocked into the river) but she figured it out. You just had to ring the bell at the same time as you pedaled and knocked the little gear lever forward, and then . . . WHOOSH, the bike's front wheel lifted from the ground, the wind smacked you in the face, and you were flying. Actually flying!

Despite the horrible things that were going on, she still grinned like a dog with its head out a car window. Unfortunately, it was only as the borrowed post bike cleared the rooftops that Tarkus discovered he was scared of heights. Or at least, scared of heights experienced from the back of a badly piloted, wobbly, flying bike, anyway.

"AAAAAAAARGGGHHHH! GO DOWN, GO DOWN."

"I'M TRYING!"

"AAAAAARGGGHH!"

"You're going to make me deaf, just shut up!"

They whizzed through the cool night air over London, straight through the level of flying folk she'd seen earlier. Around them spun witches, bats, owls, and some straight-up massive moths. Emily hadn't mastered steering yet, so they kept cutting across other people's flight paths, leaving a trail of angry, fist-waving ladies in pointy hats. She was now just shouting "sorry" continually to save time. A curse zinged past her head after the last near-miss, and she was struggling to straighten the bike up. Tarkus wailing behind her and clutching at her every time she cornered wasn't helping.

"You're going to strangle me. Again!"

"Would that make this stop?"

The moon-silvered streak of river below had been leading them to Big Ben, but the steering problems meant she'd gone way off course. She was now just trying to head in the direction of the green light. At last, she spotted a landmark she recognized . . . and came very close to running straight into it.

"Sorry, Nelson," she said as they skimmed over the admiral's hat. She angled the bike down and took the direct route down Whitehall from Trafalgar Square.

"Look, there it is. We're nearly there." She pointed ahead and the bike wobbled. There was a groan from behind.

"I'm not opening my eyes!"

Big Ben, the Great Working, loomed before them, a pointed tower of sandy stone jutting above the other huge buildings of Westminster. It rippled with power as the emerald magic energy coruscated over it. She put the bike into a steep, arcing turn to bring them around in front of it and then . . .

"Erm, so, if you didn't know how to land one of these, how would you figure it out?"

"AAAAAARGGGHH!"

"You've got to stop that!"

She stopped pedaling and, with great care, tweaked the brakes. The bike dropped out of the air like a stone. This time they both screamed. It fell down and down, the lights of the tower blurring into lines, the wind ripping away the sound of their screams. She forced her hand to unclamp from the brake lever and heaved at the pedals. Just when they were about to smash into the ground, the bike leveled out and flew forward again, skimming the cobbles but never touching. They whizzed at a phenomenal speed through the courtyard of Parliament. When a black-clad figure leapt out in front of them, it was too late to swerve.

"Look out, look out!"

There was a sickening crunch as they collided, then they were spinning in the air, sailing from the bike and smacking the ground, tumbling to a halt as the bike smashed on the stones. Emily lay still. Was she alive? She sat up and groaned. Sadly, yes. She patted herself all over; nothing was broken, and the Hog wasn't flat. She was really dizzy, though; what just happened? Her head stopped spinning and it all came back. That horrible crunching noise. Oh no. She crawled to her feet as Tarkus, who lay near her, did the same. He limped over to the squashed figure on the cobbles behind them.

"Are they . . ."

"He's Dead," said Tarkus.

"Oh god." Emily tried not to throw up.

"No, I mean he was Dead to start with, so don't worry."

"Eh?"

Emily limped over to where Tarkus was kneeling by the body. She leaned over the bashed-up mess the bike had left.

"Hang on, that's flippin' fang-face."

Lord Peregrine Stabville-Chest, the ultimate predator of the night, lay twitching on the ground. Along with the hoof-print and the rhino hole, he now had a tire mark from his chest to the top of his pushed-in head. He groaned and jerked one hand. It was about the only part of him that wasn't damaged.

"He tried to eat me!" said Emily.

"And you parked a bike on his head. I think you're even." Tarkus knelt, pulled his silver handcuffs out, and clipped Peregrine's wrist to a nearby lamppost. "This'll stop him changing shape and getting away until we come back."

"If *he's* here . . ." said Emily.

"Then she must be, too. You were right."

The huge edifice of the clock tower loomed over them, pulsing with light.

"The main mechanism is up at the top. She'll be there," said Emily, shading her eyes as she looked. "Shall we go up on the bike?"

"I would rather milk a dragon. We'll take the stairs. Now . . ."

He turned to her, face taut with worry. "If the vampire was here, then others may be, too. It'll be dangerous, so you should stay—"

"Oh, don't you dare!" said Emily, lip quivering with rage. "Don't you dare. This whole thing is dangerous, and my mom's up there, I just know it."

"I was just going to say, stay back and let me handle the Bear, and you deal with the Nocturne. You're immune to her influence, after all."

"Oh. I see. Sorry, I just thought . . ."

"You didn't think at all. Maybe you should start, once in a while."

Burn. She didn't even have a comeback.

He got his second-best truncheon out from his belt and limped off across the courtyard, toward the huge door of the main building.

She caught up with him at the door. It was cracked open. Tarkus was peering in, his lips pursed.

Inside were a number of guards in red-and-black uniforms. They were all lined up along the sides of the hall, facing the wall and marching on the spot, staring into space. Around them hovered the swirl of the Nocturne's music, and their feet moved in time to her distant drum.

"So much for the elite battalion of combat sorcerers, then," he said.

"Are they okay?"

"They're enchanted. There's nothing we can do."

They picked their way past them, through the stunning architecture of the hall and toward the little brown wooden door that said "Clock Tower." It would have been quaint if it hadn't been hanging half ripped off its hinges. The claw marks on it told them who else was here. Tarkus took a deep breath and nodded to himself.

"Ready?"

"Hang on, I just want to try something one more time." As she spoke, she pulled a piece of paper and a pen out of her bag and, after uncapping the pen with her teeth, she scribbled a few sentences onto the paper, then left it on the floor.

"What are you going to do with that?"

"Nothing. That was it."

He squinted at her, shook his head, then went into the clock tower. "I'll go first, try and stay some way behind me."

"Why?"

"So they can't get us both at the same time."

"Oh."

Her stomach was knotting as they reached the bottom of the stairs. It was a spiral staircase with a black iron bannister. The central well hole went up too far to see all the way to the top. Long, thick white ropes dangled down the middle. They were like the bell ropes in church towers, but were probably for hauling things up with.

"Come on. Best if we don't talk," he said. He turned to go but she grabbed his arm and pulled him back into a fierce hug. He stood very still, then awkwardly patted her back.

"Thank you for coming with me. Be careful," she said, then let him go. As she did, a lilac scent filled the space between them. He flushed, stuttered, and turned back to the stairs.

She followed a good ten steps behind him and was soon having trouble staying even that close. His longer legs were a definite advantage, and the curving spiral climb went on forever. She'd been counting steps but had given up after two hundred. The inside of the staircase was lit by tall thin windows set into the outer wall. The flickering light of intense magic from outside filled the stairwell with moving shadows. She'd leaned out over the rail just once and had been glad it was dark. It was a long, long way down. The crackle of magic drowned all other noises out, and she just had the endless plod of feet on stairs to keep her company.

As she walked she tried to reach inside herself for whatever magic she had. Using it by accident had given her the way into it: a little twist of something different in her, the thing that turned to liquid in her chest when she changed or wiggled away. What was she going to do with it? What use was being a hare? She could nibble them, she supposed. Destroy their salads. She was thinking about this when a stench filled the stairwell. Not the clean, floral perfume of Tarkus, but a dank, sour odor. It reeked of old blood and meat, of dog breath and rusting iron. It was the vile smell of the . . .

"Bear," whispered Tarkus, as the menacing furry bulk of him appeared above them. In the small stairwell, he was so huge the bannister only came up to just over his knees. He was halfway between his forms, face all distended with teeth.

"Children sneaking, think Bear not smell you?"

He grinned and took a step down.

"Mistress not need you now. Bear can play." He grinned wider and his nose started to stick out more. "Soon Bear play outside in Daylight, too, but you will be appetizer."

"I will give you one chance to surrender, sir," said a clear voice. Tarkus had strode up a step, second-best truncheon in hand. Emily groaned. The Bear's grin widened further.

"Remember you, stupid police boy. You are joke."

"I am an officer in good standing of the Night Watch, and you are under arrest."

What was he thinking? She was going to get him killed.

"Hurgh hurgh hurgh. Joke good, but not save you this time." The Bear took another step down toward them. "Bear eat you, then eat Pooka girl."

He licked his lips.

"No, that's not going to happen," said Tarkus. He had the same pale but determined look as the last time he'd faced the Bear. Which had ended so well.

"And how will you stop Bear, tiny meat snack?"

Another step down. Tarkus stood firm.

"I've thought about this. You followed her all around London with your amazing nose."

"Bear has best sense of smell in world, stupid police boy. Will smell your blood next."

As he spoke his words became a growl and the change was complete. He was all bear now.

To Emily's horror, Tarkus started to walk up the steps. She tried to grasp at her Pooka magic to help him, but it wiggled away from her as she panicked.

"My name is not 'police boy,'" he said with dignity. "My name is Constable-in-Training Tarkus Poswa."

The Bear threw his paws up high and came charging down the stairs, roaring.

"And you, sir, can SMELL THIS!"

Tarkus dropped his truncheon and with a push of both hands unleashed a tidal wave of scent. In one blast came every fragrance he had inside him. Pepper and flowers, perfume and spices, herbs and aromatics. It was a chaotic brew of intense odors and drifting, maddening aromas. For Emily, farther down the stairs, it was overwhelming. To the Bear's sensitive nose, it was an explosion. His charge turned into a stagger backward, and he cannoned off the stairwell wall, clutching his nose with both paws, roaring and howling in outrage. As the Bear swayed, blinded and confused, Tarkus did something beyond stupid. He ran up the stairs toward where the Bear howled and flailed and clawed at itself. He ducked under one huge razor-tipped paw and, as the Bear turned away toward the bannister, he threw himself into the tiny gap between Bear and wall and, bracing himself, he *pushed*!

It would never have worked anywhere else. The Bear must have been five times heavier than him, but here in this little stairway, with the Bear off balance, and the bannister so low and close to his knees, Tarkus tipped him just enough. As the Bear teetered Tarkus threw everything he had into it, letting loose an animal roar himself, pushing with all his might. The Bear toppled over the bannister with a terrible howl, clawing for a grip as it went. It didn't find one, but its claws did find Tarkus. As the Bear dropped, a razor-tipped paw lashed Tarkus's arm and pulled him over, too. He went without a noise, and they plunged down into the void straight past Emily's appalled face. A series of awful crashes echoed up, as they hit every metal rail and stone edge on the way down to the floor far below.

CHAPTER 24

Emily hurled herself toward the bannister. Oh thank god. There was Tarkus, much farther down, clinging to a thick white rope with just one arm, and dangling over the void. Of the Bear, there was no sign.

"Hang on, I'm coming!" she yelled and ran down the stairs. She got level with him and, not daring to look down, stretched out to grab the rope and pull it in to the side of the stairs. He groaned as she did, gripping the rope with one arm and his knees, his other arm flapping uselessly at his side and dripping blood down into the long, empty drop beneath them. She pulled the heavy rope in toward her and he slid down as she did. He was going to fall, but she clawed at his uniform, and then with a lurch and a shriek he was tumbling over the bannister and on top of her. They ended up in a heap a few steps down, with Tarkus clutching his arm and moaning.

"Are you okay?"

"You're kneeling on me." His voice was muffled as his cape was over his head.

"Oh, sorry. Here." She shuffled out of the way and sat on the next step up. He tried to stand, but then collapsed back down, clutching his arm and side.

"Hecate's claws," he snarled through clenched teeth. "I think I've broken something. Possibly several somethings." He slumped against the wall.

"That was the stupidest thing I've ever seen," Emily said.

"Oh," he said.

"And the bravest."

He smiled.

"I can't move, you'll have to—"

"Yep, I'm going now, will you be okay?"

"I'll be fine. Good fortune, Emily Featherhaugh."

"Just hang on and I'll be back soon. Here." She rooted around in her pocket. "Can you take Hoggins? This could get nasty."

She rubbed noses with the Hog, who was doing a wrinkled face of displeasure at this idea.

"Look after this idiot for me, Hoggins. I'll be back, I

promise." She passed him to Tarkus, gave them both her bravest smile, and turned to go.

She walked a few steps up, then paused. "Seriously, though, 'Smell this'? That's what you came up with?"

"It was a fraught moment."

"Imagine if those had been your last words? Ha! Smell you later, Violet." And with that she was off up to the darkness at the top of the stairs.

She heard her mom before seeing her. Standard. The loud, snarky voice echoing down the stairwell from an open door on the final landing above.

"Y'know, I just don't feel like it. Sure and why don't you have a go?"

Her heart pounded, and she crept up the final steps on the tips of her toes. A pulse of music, half heard, came from the same direction, then the voice she'd never forget.

"You know that even I am vulnerable to their aura. You will do it for me."

"Ye reckon?"

"They must be positioned carefully on the pendulum. So you will do it, and you will free us all."

Emily edged her head around the open door. The Nocturne stood inside, her back toward her, then over on the other side . . . her mom! Her dreadful, embarrassing, glorious, secret agent Pooka Mom! She was in a dirty T-shirt and jeans, tattooed arms linked together with a thick set of silver cuffs with a chain between them. Her face was bruised, but she was grinning like she didn't have a care in the world. She was leaning against the corner of a great big piece of clockwork machinery that could have been an upside-down steam train: the clock's main mechanism, all cogs and wheels and gears and sticky-out brass bits. At her feet was the small silver box, open on the floor, with the bad pennies gleaming inside.

"Free youse, ye mean. Everyone else is fine."

"Don't you long to gallop outside again? To taunt and trick the Day Folk once more?" The Nocturne's voice was low and urgent, and it was underlined with a deep musical tone that throbbed through Emily's bones. "Do this, unchain the spell, and we will be glorious again."

"Yer nonsense don't work on me, love, you should know that." Her mom's grin grew more insolent. "The only glory this is about is yers. The rest of 'em won't last a year. Do ye actually want a war?"

"I WANT TO FEED!" The shout made Emily flinch. "NO more scraps of stolen music barely keeping me together. NO more fading away. I will reclaim my world and feast, and if all the Night Folk have to burn for me to do it, then so be it."

"I'm going to be honest, ye're not selling it."

"Enough of you, Pooka. You will kneel."

"Yeah, not famous for that." Her mom straightened up, rolled her shoulders, and stared at the Nocturne. She wasn't smiling anymore.

"So then, the old-fashioned way." The Nocturne had her back turned to Emily, but the cold blue light of her eyes colored the air around her. "Do it, or I will tear everything you love apart."

"Ye–"

"You know we have your husband, but now we have the coins. Who did they come from?"

Her mom's eye twitched, but she didn't speak. The Nocturne spread her arms wide and softened her voice.

"Your Emily. Your precious girl."

Emily's mom's face tightened in anger. "Ye're bluffing," she said. "I won't do it." But her voice wavered as she spoke.

"Would you test me? Truly?" The Nocturne seemed to suck the light from the air around her, standing in shadows lit by the blaze of her eyes. "You saw what I did to my own sister. Think what I will do to your girl."

The two women stared at each other in silence and it was Emily's mom who broke first. Her head dropped, and she reached for the necklace of bad pennies in the box and picked them up. She unclipped the clasp, then held the ends in her hands for the space of a few breaths. She closed her eyes, a tear ran down her cheek, and she let the pennies fall, clinking one by one, off the chain and into the box.

"Ye swear ye won't hurt her. Or Alan?"

"Once you do this, no harm shall come to them by my hand."

"We both know that's hardly good enough." There was a little flare of anger in her mom's voice, but she looked beaten.

"We both know you have no choice."

Her mom reached down to the box and picked a single coin out. Face emotionless now, she turned and moved to a long, tube-shaped weight dangling from a chain near the edge of the machine. Emily recognized it from her research; it was the main time-keeping pendulum of the whole mechanism. On the top of it was the bronze gleam of old coins. The timing pennies Emily had read about—tiny, careful weights to keep the clock in order. Emily's mom leaned in and held the bad penny over the pendulum—a small, dangerous weight that could send the Great Working into chaos. The Nocturne moved closer, face exultant and inhuman.

"Yes."

Far above her, there was a harmonic vibration, a pregnant, imminent ripple of sound from a giant bell frozen in the act of ringing, now on the brink of release.

Her mom's hand hovered over the pendulum.

"Do it. Weaken the charm, and I will do the rest. As soon as there is a chime, there is music I can wield." The Nocturne's voice was a sibilant whisper. "Think of the child. Place the coin."

Her mom closed her eyes and . . .

"Mom, no!" Emily jumped out of hiding and ran into the room. "She's lying! I'm okay."

Her mom went white.

"What are you doing here? Run!"

There was a blur of blue and the Nocturne stood behind Emily, gripping her by the neck with a frigid hand.

"You make bluff into reality, you ridiculous child." The cold grip on her neck tightened with an inhuman strength, and pain rippled through her. "Now, Pooka, if you don't do what I say, I will show you what tearing apart looks like."

Her mom squawked. Emily gritted her teeth, closed her eyes, and reached for whatever she truly was. Not letting it take her in panic this time, but claiming it. She found it, held it, and as the clawlike nails dug into her throat, she exhaled and let the loose liquid sensation in her chest flow out to fill her whole being. She became energy. Her other forms were here: a glimpse of sharp teeth and big paws, of a flying mane and sleek forequarters, but beyond her reach this time. Instead she reached for the form she'd already become. She opened the wrapper of the thick muscular back legs, twitching nose, long, lean back, and magnificent ears, and poured herself in, fitting inside the hare, *being* the hare, and it was the most natural thing in the world.

Her new form wasn't being gripped by the throat by steel-strong hands. Instead, it was scrabbling at the front of a blue velvet dress, doing some satisfying scratching and biting. The Nocturne cried out as Emily lashed out at her face with teeth and nails, then kicked out hard with her powerful back legs. She bounded onto the floor, skidding on the polished wood, whirling around the Nocturne once in a circle, then accelerating away in a streak to where her mom was standing by the huge clockwork engine. She reached it while the Nocturne was still clutching at her face and whirling around to see where the hare had gone behind her. Emily concentrated, her little hare face all screwed up and paws tensed, and then, with a shudder and a sneeze, she was herself again.

"Urgh. Oh god, that's so wrong."

She ignored the wave of sickness that passed over her, and grabbed the box with the slew of coins spread over its velvet lining, snapping it shut and stuffing it inside her coat. Her mom, for once, was speechless.

"Mom, let's go! Run."

She reached out and grabbed her mom's hand, the edge of the silver handcuffs burning her wrist as she did, and yanked her through the door, kicking it shut behind them. They ran as a steam whistle of anger hissed from the Nocturne, and panes of glass cracked all around the room.

"CHILD!"

They skittered onto the landing, and Emily turned to go down, but her mom tugged her across toward the next set of stairs up.

"But?"

"We can't outrun her—she'll be straight on us. Come on."

They hammered up the stairs as the door splintered behind them, then a whir of blue movement erupted out of the room they'd fled. By then, they were through a big door at the top of the stairs, and her mom had slammed it and was tipping up benches to block it. She was really strong. Crikey.

"Grab anything ye can. It won't hold her, but it might give me a chance to get these cuffs off of me."

Using all her weight, Emily shoved a big cupboard of tools across the door and piled wooden crates of clockwork cogs up against it, too. Outside, something that sounded way bigger and heavier than the petite Nocturne slammed into the door.

"And don't think I haven't noticed this is a school night," said her mom as she wedged herself against the heaving barricade.

"Oh come on!" said Emily.

"Ha! Come here." She swept Emily into an awkward,

handcuffed side-hug, and they squeezed each other until Emily squeaked.

"You're loving me too tight!"

"Sorry, darl."

Emily squeezed out for a breather, and her mom looked her up and down as the barricade rang with blows and dark music from outside.

"Well, look at yerself." She curled her lip. "I can feel a short and intensely painful conversation with my eejit brother coming on."

"Oh, you can talk. I need to—Whoa!"

She had looked around the room for the first time since she'd come in.

It was vast and square, and each of the walls was another huge square of white glass with the backward numbers of a clock face on it, lit by a circle of gas lamps and a crackle of occult fire from outside. From a vast clockwork mechanism in the center of the room, a system of rods and chains connected to the middle of each of the backward clock faces, and the huge hands silhouetted against the outside. All of them pointed straight up to show midnight. The whole mechanism was motionless and silent, but it throbbed with contained power and rippled with movement as the emerald actinic light made shadows dance across it. She was behind the clock faces at the very top of the tower. High above her were the dangling forms of immense bells, like five monstrous metal bats in the belfry. A quarter bell in each corner and one huge bell right in the middle—the real Big Ben.

"Cor."

"S'good, ain't it? I remember them building it," said her mom, braced against the stack of furniture. It shuddered as heavy impacts and bursts of deep, bassy sound rocked the whole pile and made Emily's back teeth and ears throb.

"Now stop being a tourist and find something to get these cuffs off. I can't change with silver on me."

Emily had a million questions she wanted to ask, especially the one about what year her mom's birthday was. Instead she tore around the clock room and came back with a giant wrench. As she got back, the impacts on the door stopped and silence fell.

"Erm, do you think she's gone? Only, I left my friend Tarkus out there and he's got a broken . . ."

A new sound came from outside. A steady, throbbing drumbeat, a deep and primitive rhythm with a guttural chant over it. It sounded old and dark and dangerous. Hunting music. Killing music.

"Oh, that's never good," said her mom.

CHAPTER 25

Emily's mom's face drained of color.

"We've got to get these cuffs off, so I can fight."

"What? What's she doing?"

"One thing at a time."

She gestured at the big wrench Emily was holding.

"I need you to hit these as hard as you can." She braced the chain between the cuffs against a metal shelf edge. "Quick."

CLANG!

"That's it, hit it again."

CLANG!

The shelf buckled as she did, and the cuffs gleamed, undented.

"Dammit. Again!"

The sound from outside grew louder, and now the thrumming vibration was joined by the sound of something bigger beating at the door. The barricade shuddered under the blows.

"Okay, this isn't working." Her mom grimaced. "When she gets in, I'll lead her up to the belfry and ye leg it."

"No, I'm not leaving you."

The sound reached a pitch, and the door and the barricade were smashed open, tumbling them both out of the way.

The Nocturne strode into the room through the wreckage, and Emily gasped. She was transformed, all traces of the beautiful gentlewoman now gone. She resembled one of those big curvy carvings of the old cave goddesses, just with more horrible scary bits. She was twice or perhaps three times the size she had been. Her dress hung in tatters around her, and her body and head were swollen with an inner fire that stretched and blackened her skin, bulking her into a nightmare figure. She glowed like metal heated in a forge, and stunk of iron and blood. Her eyes were a storm of rage and light, and her face was terrible to behold.

The music throbbed and pulsed around her, all modern sophistication gone, just raw animal rhythms that made Emily's whole head buzz. It was all too possible to picture the awful things that had been done in her name when her music had pounded long ago.

"You thought you could challenge me?" The Nocturne's

voice was deep and raw. "I am greater than you. I am greater than all. I was here first, and I shall be the last thing ever, as the final heartbeat of your ridiculous species fades out. Now bring me my COINS!"

Emily's mom got to her feet, hands still cuffed, but fists clenched and teeth bared.

"Right," her mom whispered out of the corner of her mouth. "She's monologuing. The Older Powers always do that. We get one chance. I'll jump her, and ye leg it."

"I said I'm not leaving you!"

"Have you followed me to the heart of Midnight just to have a fight?" Her mom shook her head in wonder. "I want ye out safe."

"I'm staying. There's nowhere to go, anyway!"

"Eejit. Can you change?"

Emily strained at the new sort-of muscle she had found within, thinking hare-shaped thoughts, but got nothing but a headache for her trouble.

"No, I'm sorry, I'm too tired."

"Best keep hold of that wrench, then."

The Nocturne was still ranting, spitting venom and bile, and working herself into a froth. She was still getting bigger, too. Emily's mom edged around the room, Emily behind her, keeping the clockwork in the middle between them and the thing.

"I–I did have a plan to get help," Emily said in a quiet voice. "But I don't think it's worked. I'm so sorry. I'm sorry for everything."

"Never mind. If there's a chance, love, get down the stairs." Her mom didn't turn away from the monstrous thing in front of them, but reached back and squeezed her hand, hard. "Please."

"Okay."

The music stopped.

"Enough whispering, animals. It's time for you to die."

"I love ye, sweetheart," her mom said and, grabbing a long iron winding rod leaned against the clockwork stack, she stepped out to confront the Nocturne. "Ah, shut yer trap and get on with it, ye wagon."

The Nocturne growled and knuckled forward, the music rising up again, one huge arm reaching out toward the tiny form holding an iron bar. Emily burned and froze at the same time. How had they ended up here?

A small but distinct clearing of a tiny throat cut through all the noise. The Nocturne's heavy head swung around as she sought out the sound. Emily's mom let out a low whistle in shock. On the floor between them was a tiny, round, prickly, brown figure.

"Hog! How did you . . . ?"

The Hog did not look back, but shuffled forward, raised

his little face, squinted his small eyes, and gave the Nocturne a distinctly old-fashioned look. She leaned over to see.

"And what are . . . YOU!"

She took a step back. Her music slowed and her chest trembled with emotion. Was she going to stop?

"NO! Not this time! I defy your law. I will be free!"

She drew herself up, the edges of her now licked with a black fire, and raised her club-like hands to smash all before her.

"Not my Hoggins!" screeched Emily, and she leapt and skidded past her mom, sliding on her knees and grabbing the Hog as she did, just before the huge hands crashed down where he had been. She slid past and smashed into the wall, rolling over and crawling away, with the Hog spiked into one hand.

"Ow ow prickly prickly!"

Behind her the monster closed in, hands raised to smash once more. There was a distinct thud as Emily's mom whanged the Nocturne with her iron bar. It distracted the monster just long enough to turn around and knock Emily's mom across the room with a backhanded blow, where she hit the floor and didn't get up.

"Mom!" screamed Emily, and then the Nocturne was upon her.

"You! You enrage me!"

"You're not the first person to say that," she said, because her gob would apparently not quit, even now.

"No more."

The Nocturne raised her terrible fists, and in Emily's hand the Hog squirmed and moved and popped his head out. There was a heat in her palm and an unusual wriggle from him and—

A big black bike crashed through the glass of one of the clock faces. A familiar face was crouched at the handlebars, and a larger form bent over him, clutching at his waist. The bike skidded to a halt and her dad—her boring, quiet, composting dad—threw himself off it, tucked his shoulder in as he landed, and forward-rolled up onto his feet, drawing a flaming sword, which he held in a professional two-handed grip.

"Get away from her, you beast," he snarled. He spared a wink for an astonished Emily and said in more normal tones, "Thanks for the rescue party, Puzzle. The Bloody Mary brought them straight to me. Japonica sends her regards."

The other figure unfolded itself from the bike and stood tall; long dark hair spilling over a tattered white dress. The Library stepped between Emily and the Nocturne, and Emily noticed that as well as newly black hair, she had both slippers on. There was a small sigh from the Hog, and he curled back into her hand.

"You!" The Nocturne staggered back. "But you have no power!"

That wasn't true. The Library crackled with energy. "Oh, but I do. I *do*. I am full of boarding schools and faraway trees, and wizards, and heroes, and romance, and talking animals, and poetry." She was giggling with joy. "I am fizzbanged with energy and the new. I have feasted!"

"But how . . . ?"

The Library turned her head to Emily and, was that a smile?

"A brave child gave me a gift. All of her books from outside. New work, new words, new LIFE."

She held up glowing hands to the Nocturne.

"She made me strong again, then wrote to tell me of your ill-thought schemes. I am here to make good our vow to save the Night Folk, sister."

"No! It was your vow to rot in this prison. I will be free!"

"We *are* free. It is outside that is the trap; here we keep both worlds alive." The Library's voice was full of sympathy.

Emily's dad glanced over at her mom, who was groping her way up from the floor. He whistled sharply in a two-tone little tune, and without taking his eyes off the Nocturne, he reached in his pocket, and lobbed something over his shoulder.

"Maeve! Key!" he shouted.

Emily's mom's hands shot up, silver cuffs glinting, and snatched the key from the air. There was a rapid clicking, a clink as the silver hit the floor, then in a sudden expanding shadow her mom exploded up from the floor as a *very* angry black horse. She reared and snorted her rage. Her red eyes flared with fire as she gained purchase on the floor and galloped across. Her mom braked just before hitting the Nocturne, and reared up at her dad's side, front hooves lashing the air. Her dad grinned, flame-licked sword held high.

"I told you to get away from her," he said.

"No, no, no!" Beneath the Nocturne's skin something roiled and moved, and the music that surrounded them shrieked with discord. The Library took a step forward, too, hands held out, palms glowing white, with a flicker of black on them as words moved beneath her skin. As the Dangerous Deliveries Specialist and the Library advanced, and the Pooka reared and screamed in fury, the Nocturne took first one, then another ponderous step back. As the sword blazed and the Library glowed brighter, the black fire that had flickered over the Nocturne faded, and she shrank back to her smaller size.

"Come, sister, come with me. It's not too late. We can find a way together now. We do not have to go gently into that good night anymore." The Library didn't smile, but her eyes were kind. "Surely you can see that?"

The Nocturne's face flickered from rage to a sadness so naked it made Emily's heart hurt.

"Together?"

Her voice was fading, the constant music starting to play out of tune. The Library said nothing but held out her hand. Emily's mom's front legs touched back down on the floor, but her lips were still peeled back from her teeth, and her dad held the sword ready to strike.

The Nocturne, a pale woman again, in the tatters of her dress, reached out to the Library. She hesitated then ... grabbed her by the wrist, not the hand. Her eyes flared, midnight blue.

"No. I will have it all or no one will. I will not be CONTAINED!"

The Library tried to pull back, Emily's mom reared up, and her dad shot forward swinging his blade. The Nocturne threw her head back and shrieked. It was the loudest noise in history, it contained every note ever sung, and the primal music of rockslides, howling storms, and cracking ice floes. It filled the room and their heads until it was unbearable. Her dad was flung away, her mom crashed to the ground, and the Library slumped to her knees, her light fading. Emily curled up in a ball, hedgehog-style, and held the Hog close to her face. She would have sworn she was going to go mad or die, then the Hog wriggled and her ears popped, and the music was quieter than it had been. Still awful, but just about bearable.

When it finally stopped, she uncurled. Every face of the clock had cracked. Her mom and dad lay unmoving, his hand flung out toward her, his sword guttering out next to him. The Nocturne stood over the Library where she knelt swaying on the floor, her hair streaked with white again, and with eyes as lost as they had been when Emily first met her.

"I was always stronger, sister. You should have remembered." The Nocturne turned to Emily and lurched as she did. Her hair was now gray all over, her face pinched and drawn, all beauty fled. Whatever she had just done had cost her dearly.

"Still with us? You're made of stern stuff. Give me what I desire, and I might let you live."

Emily levered herself up off the floor, and her hand found the cool silver of the box inside her jacket.

"If I do, you've got to let everyone go."

The Nocturne snarled.

"We've bargained this already, and you've broken your half. I'll do as I please."

"All right, all right, what if I put the pennies on the pendulum for you? Will you let them go then?" She inched closer to the blue-draped figure.

"Interesting. We can barter it perhaps. But first, hand me the prize."

"Not unless you agree."

"No!" The words came in a moan, from the Library, whose legs wouldn't work to hold her up. "She doesn't understand. It's the end of everything."

Emily bit the inside of her lip and took another small step toward the Nocturne. She held the box out, and the piercing blue gaze followed it.

"Agreed?"

"Not agreed. No more warnings. Return them." The pallid face was made a skull by jade light and flickering shadows.

"You want them? Then here you go."

She was close enough. She snapped the box open and flicked the loose coins all over the Nocturne. The thirty coins hit her straight in the face, chest, and body, and slid down the front of the remains of her dress. Not a single one slipped off, instead they all lodged where they fell—in her hair, against her skin, inside the tattered fabric. It was remarkably unlucky considering.

The Nocturne's blue eyes widened, and she shrieked as though the pennies were white-hot. This time her shriek sounded human and scared. She began to claw at herself, hopping up and down on one foot, scratching at her chest, and digging down the front of her dress. It was a pretty good impression of a mad, self-grooming monkey and Emily had to laugh. The Nocturne snarled.

"You will pay for—"

She didn't finish her sentence as, in rapid succession, she stepped through a previously unnoticed rotten floorboard up to her knee, and then stumbled straight into the path of a loose spring that picked that very second to snap off from the clockwork and ricochet right into her face. As she clawed at it, one of the quarter bells, smaller than Big Ben but still bigger than a car, unexpectedly rusted through and smashed down on top of her, crushing her through the floor with a squeak and a bong. What rotten luck.

"Blimey," said Emily.

From below came a series of bangs, clangs, screams, and bursts of very loud music of all different types. It suggested a series of terribly unfortunate events befalling one person, one after another. Although it all sounded awfully painful, it was difficult for Emily not to smile. There was a final, awful throbbing note of music, then an out-of-tune howl that ended in the flat, clapping sound of air rushing in to fill an empty space. A waft of acrid black smoke drifted up through the hole in the floor.

The last note of night music had been played. The Nocturne was finished.

EPILOGUE

In the aftermath of the Battle of Big Ben, as it became
known (mainly by Emily), lots of things happened. Emily
helped her shaky dad over to where her mom lay flat out
on the floor, human again. His hand was warm on Emily's
arm, and his face was still his face, whether it was lit by a
flaming sword or not. When they got to her mom, the muffled words of one of her drinking songs were drifting up from
under her multicolored mop of hair.

"Mom?"

"What, I'm awake. I'm just going to the shop—Oh!" She
sat up, dazed, then grinned. "How ya, loves? All sorted,
right?"

"All sorted." Emily threw herself down and hugged her.

"Ah, I knew it would be. These things usually turn out fine."

Her dad knelt in close, too, shaking his head as she spoke, and gathering them both into his arms.

"Uh-huh. 'Famously uncatchable,' I believe you said?"

"Ah, ye can't go 'round believing everything I say, ye know. We're a very unreliable people." She grinned. "Anyways, didn't ye manage to get caught, too, Mr. Danger?"

He sighed, but smiled as he did.

"That's Mr. Dangerous Deliveries to you. I was set upon from behind while trying to rescue you, in fact."

"Oh, and that'll be my fault, I suppose—"

He shut her up by kissing her, and Emily didn't even mind.

Having given the Hog a severe telling-off ("Mr. H. Oggins, you have been *very* naughty. What were you thinking?"), she kissed his nose and popped him back in her pocket and they all went down to find Tarkus. He was still propped up on the stairs, semiconscious, but okay. Emily made him a daffodil and chip sandwich and sat with him while healing witches were called. He was soon carried down by a squad of the Night Watch, including, to Emily's astonishment, a tearful-looking Sarge (who proved to Emily's further surprise to be two feet tall, and made principally of ivy). There was even talk of a promotion.

The Bear had vanished, leaving behind only an enormous dent in the floor.

Of the Nocturne there was no sign, either, apart from a cracked quarter bell, the shreds of a blue dress, and a scattered pile of coins. Emily helped to pick them up and thread them back onto the necklace, but wouldn't have sworn they were all there. She and her mom both counted them but never got to the same number twice.

"Cursed things," said her mom. "They're the devil's own job to keep hold of."

"The Nocturne, is she, well, you know . . ." Emily trailed off. Despite everything, it wasn't a nice thought.

A deep voice answered her from behind. "Dead? No, you cannot kill my kind that way. We're more idea than flesh." The Library drifted into the room. "You have weakened her significantly, but I fear she will be back."

The Library was fizzing less now after the battle but was again clear-eyed and present.

"Ello, booky. Ye look grand." Her mom grinned.

The Library raised one perfect black eyebrow but did not comment. She held out a hand to Emily. She really was flippin' tall.

"I thank you for your gift, Emily Featherhaugh. I have one for you in turn."

"Cor, is it a medal?"

"It is . . . a Library card."

"Riiiight."

"Then she ran off with me *and* my heart."

They were sitting in the battered living room back at home, drinking hot chocolate as the Hog pottered around the coffee table, nosing for scraps from the sandwich plate. Her mom and dad were giving her "the talk" about their life. Their *real* life.

"Wait. Mom, you were a horse when you met Dad?"

"It was more complicated than that, darl."

"You married a horse?"

"Well . . ."

"Wait, does this mean I'm half horse? Am I, like, a foal, or something? Or a shire?"

"Shire horses are the massive bulky ones. As you saw, your mother is a sleek, well-proportioned animal when she's a horse."

"So, I'm a pony. A Shetland pony with no friends."

"Ah, that's never true. Ye've got the Hog for one, and all his fleas, too. Sure that's loads of friends."

"MOM!"

Her mom grinned, pleased with herself, and pantomimed scratching a lot. Emily sighed. Her dad hid a grin as he sipped his tea. He was still quiet now they were home, but Emily was starting to understand that. He had a VERY stressful job.

"So, I've been wanting to ask, is the Hog magic or what? Did you send him with me because you knew I might need help?"

"Can I?" Her mom leaned forward to where the Hog chumbled around on the table.

"'Course."

"I was talking to him."

Her mom picked the Hog up. She inclined her head with great politeness, took a long look at him, dipped her head once more, and placed him back in Emily's hand.

"Nah. Never seen him before in me life. He's just a hedgepig. Although . . ." She leaned in to look at him again and smiled. ". . . a very handsome and wise one."

The Hog made a contented little piggly grunt and shuffled his spines. Emily narrowed her eyes at the pair of them.

"But . . ."

"Nope, just a hedgepig." Her mom stood up. "Don't forget I'm going to teach ye how to turn into a hound later this week. Keep Friday night free." She then vanished off to her studio, as if that was an acceptable way to finish a conversation. Emily brought the Hog up, nose to nose, and gave him a long, hard look.

"Just a hedgepig, huh?"

The Hog scratched vigorously at his side (Emily was sure she saw something jump away from the spot) then turned around once in her palm, settled down, and began to snore.

"Hmmmm."

⌒ CODA ⌒

And there within the clock, rolled out of sight by pure bad luck, sits one coin that wasn't there before, rocking between two cogs, not far from the balancing beam that holds the world in order. It gleams silver and black, and glows a little in the dark.

It rubs, just a touch, inside the most carefully measured device in all of the worlds, and for every second its malign presence is there, the clock comes a tiny, infinitesimal bit closer to ticking again. Frozen time becomes a fraction of a heartbeat longer every day (for those whose hearts still beat), and somewhere the Nocturne sits, listening to a music only she can hear, and she smiles.

Soon. Soon.

ACKNOWLEDGMENTS

From Trindles:
For almost a decade, Benjamin Read has been writing me stories. For this, and a great many other things, I am deeply thankful. Creating this world together has been our biggest adventure yet and I cannot wait for the next one (I'll pack the crisp sarnies, you bring the biscuits).

My heartfelt love and appreciation goes to my husband and best friend, Chris Wildgoose. Without his bottomless supply of love, support, snacks, laughs, and excellent company, I would surely go bonkers. Thank you, thank you.

I no doubt owe a debt of gratitude to a childhood full of Mom's drawings and Dad's made-up fairy tales (with groan-worthy, puntastic titles). A very many thank-yous to them and my tribe of friends and family for their enthusiastic cheerleading.

From Read:

So many thank-yous owed, almost as many as words in the book . . .

To Rachel, who was there when it started, listened to midnight mutterings, and, most importantly, generously shared the original hogspiration who still lives in my pocket. Hog hoggity hog. (I'm totally keeping him.)

To my parents, whose endless support means the world (and especially for my dad who consistently brought luridly covered paperbacks home for an avid reader when I was wee).

To my blessed support network of friends and colleagues—Rose, Sam, Big, Zoë, Matt & Jess—who put up with my endless pencil-chewing distraction, and keep the world running around (and despite) me.

But most of all to Laura—dear friend, fellow traveler, first and ideal reader, and persistent partner-in-literary-crime—for whom many of the tales are written and without whom I would doubtless be rocking in a den made of unfinished manuscripts. May we color in between each other's lines forever more.

And from Trindles & Read, thanks to the Chickens:
To Rachel L, for helping to find the story's focus; to Elinor, for bringing it to children around the world; and to Rachel H, Myers, Jazz, and everyone else for bringing it all together.

Most of all, of course, thanks to Barry, the most excellently hatted publisher of all—for listening to a burbling extemporary rant about midnight magic from a hyperactive, hand-waving author and somehow seeing a whole world in there. Thanks for trusting us. You are the hedgehog in our publishing pocket and we will always be grateful.